Even knowing that it was there, it was difficult to see the knife handle, with the head turned into the corner of the chair. But it was evident to DeGraaf that the blade had been driven in through the temple, where the parietal bone was extremely thin. If the blade was longer than an inch or so, it would have severed so many connections in the brain that any response by Cotton would have been impossible. He would not likely have made a sound. . .

Too many suspects. Too many motives. A baffling set of fingerprints. And a denouement that establishes Barbara D'Amato as a master of the art of mystery!

## Books by Barbara D'Amato

### Cat Marsala Mysteries

Hardball
Hard Tack
Hard Luck
Hard Women
Hard Case
Hard Christmas
Hard Bargain
Hard Evidence
Hard Road

### Gerritt DeGraaf Mysteries

The Hands of Healing Murder
The Eyes on Utopia Murders

### Other Books

On My Honor

White Male Infant

Of Course You Know That Chocolate
Is a Vegetable and Other Stories

The Doctor, The Murder, The Mystery
The True Story of the Dr. John Branion Murder Case

# THE HANDS OF
# HEALING MURDER

A Dr. Gerritt DeGraaf Mystery

SPEAKING VOLUMES, LLC
NAPLES, FLORIDA
2016

The Hands of Healing Murder

ISBN 978-1-62815-245-6

For more exciting
Books, eBooks, Audiobooks and more visit us at
www.speakingvolumes.us

# THE HANDS OF HEALING MURDER

A Dr. Gerritt DeGraaf Mystery

**Barbara D'Amato**

# CHAPTER ONE

I'll say it once, but I don't want to say it again, and I certainly would never tell Gerritt: if it had not been for Gerritt DeGraaf I would never in a thousand years have solved the Cotton murder. Of course, I like to think that no one else could have solved it either.

I wouldn't admit it to DeGraaf himself, as it would ruin a nicely balanced relationship. And surely I would never mention this to the Commissioner. The Commissioner, who thinks I solved it, is very much like a badger: low to the ground, coarse hair, short legs, persistent, and nothing much above the eyebrows. Digs himself in, too. I will probably still be stuck with him twenty years from now. That's bearable. I'm good at coping with reality. But he is not the sort to confide in.

After three days on the case I had managed only to demonstrate to my own dissatisfaction that none of the eight people in the room with the corpse could have murdered him and that no one else had

1

entered. In the unsettling events that followed, De-Graaf and only DeGraaf saw the true path.

So it may seem ungrateful that I put all the patrolmen on Rush Street on the lookout for him. He rents an apartment over an Italian grocery on Rush Street. He says that his location guarantees that the smell of the air always has pleasant connotations. I left standing orders that every patrolman passing his address check for evidence that he had come back—a changed position of a curtain or shade, a light at night, an open window, anything. I was angry. He had showed me the answer, all right, but had left me holding the corpse. No details. Nothing. Not a word. I had to face the Commissioner with a handful of surmises and hot air. In view of my long record as a homicide inspector with few mental aberrations, it went off; but I was angry. DeGraaf had vanished. Left. Flew. Gringo, his colleague at the hospital, was filling in for him, but claimed not to know where he'd gone.

It was a week after he had flown, a Thursday night at 2:15 a.m., that a cop on the beat gave me a call. There was a light in DeGraaf's window. I pulled on my pants, forgot to change out of my pajama top with the red-ant print, dragged a raincoat over the whole sleepy mess, and was pounding on DeGraaf's door by 2:37.

He opened it. He was fully dressed and I could see no suitcases in the room behind him.

"Don't you know better than to open your door to a stranger at this hour?" I said. "I might have been a gang of thieves."

"I knew it was you. You have a very pudgy knock."

I walked in, studying my knuckles for fat.

"Nice to see you," said DeGraaf, leading the way back to his bar.

"You left me holding the bag," I said.

We sat on the merry-go-round horses he uses for bar stools. DeGraaf splashed whiskey into two glasses. He told me he had left me with the body and the post-mortem report, and the killer, and that was all I needed. He said, "I don't have to lead you by the hand."

"Of course not! I'm talking about the things you kept from me."

"Nothing. Not a thing."

I think I have an adequate poker face. Nevertheless, as DeGraaf stared at me, I knew he saw my anger and frustration. He had shown his own emotional reaction to the case. I think he felt sorry for me.

Quietly, without a hint of the emotion I knew he still felt, he started telling me how he had identified the killer. I must admit I had not only possessed all the facts, I had been present at most of the events.

"But the first night, the night of the murder," I said, "You were there and I wasn't."

"Of course. Through no premeditation on my part. We didn't call you until nearly midnight, because we didn't know we'd had a murder until then. But the first thing I did when you arrived was to fill you in on what had happened during the evening. Except details of atmosphere, maybe. And as I remember, you showed absolutely no interest in that sort of detail."

"Give it to me now, with the atmosphere left in."

He did, then and there, in the small hours. He knew I was angry, that I believed he should have stayed for the mopping up. But maybe he also

wanted to get the story out of his system. He filled
it in with that command of memory he uses when
he feels like it, and I have to say that he had been
fair to me from the beginning. He had played no
games. I should have known the answer that first
night. So should he, he says, but he may be trying
to make me feel better. After all, he's just a doctor.
I'm the policeman.

"The night of the bridge game at Cotton's," he
said, "was like the depths of winter, although it was
mid-April and should have felt like spring. From
that first night to the end of it, I felt as if the whole
world were cold and dark."

DeGraaf said he had been invited, to his surprise,
to Dr. Cotton's for dinner that Sunday evening. It
was planned as a formal, old-fashioned dinner party, with two tables of duplicate bridge afterward.
DeGraaf was surprised to be invited because he
knew Cotton only slightly, even though both of
them were affiliated with Hastings Hospital. De-
Graaf practiced and taught emergency room care
and trauma surgery, and was a consulting specialist
in forensic pathology for the Office of the Medical
Examiner. Cotton was a vascular surgeon. Apparently this meant they did not often meet. Their
only other connection was that Cotton's daughter
Melanie had graduated from medical school at
Northwestern University here in Chicago, where
DeGraaf taught two days a week. She had been his
student. She had gone on to become a full-time
pathologist with the Medical Examiner's office. It
was a connection, but not much of one I guess, or he
wouldn't have been so surprised at the invitation.
His curiosity got the better of him, though, and he

went to the dinner, which was his first mistake.
There had been nine at dinner, four family mem-
bers and five guests . . . .

"We will go into the library now," Dr. Adam
Cotton said. He rose from the head of the table and
left. His guests, his sister, and his daughter rose
also. All trailed obediently after him down the hall,
panelled in dark oak, to the library.

DeGraaf, who had been sitting at dinner on Melanie Cotton's right, smiled at the immediate obe-
dience everybody gave the old man. The voice
could as well have been commanding "Scalpel!"
There were people who had one persona in their
professional lives and another at home, but Cotton,
DeGraaf thought, was not one of them.

For his part, DeGraaf sauntered along contented-
ly in the wake of the crowd. He was having a fine
evening. It was the sort of house and the sort of
night that could have been transplanted from nine-
teenth century London. They had dined on roast
beef and Yorkshire pudding, a Bordeaux, and apple
pie, still hot from the oven, with cheddar cheese.
Now coffee and brandy in the library. He half expected the ladies to withdraw while the gentlemen
smoked.

The hall was oak panelled, with parquet floors of
oak. The head of a bobcat, mounted on an oak slab,
seemed to snarl perpetually from the wall. A bison's
head hung higher on the wall over the door to the
library.

The library too, was dim, but DeGraaf liked it
instantly. It was enclosed in oak bookcases, with the
exception of a fireplace at the near end and two tall
windows over shallow window seats at the far end.
One window was an inch or so ajar and the light

draft of moist cold air lightened the warmth from the fireplace. The house was a relic, not really a part of present-day Chicago.

DeGraaf set himself, standing with his back to the fire and felt content, far from the world of fast food chains and fiberboard walls. He was aware of a current of tension in the party, but could not tell where it was coming from. In any case, what did it matter? The fire blazed and at the sideboard Melanie Cotton was pouring out coffee that looked strong and black. Dr. Adam Cotton was nodding to the butler, and saying, "Johns, leave the ice on the table." The butler withdrew silently, and the library door closed after him with the discreet creak of heavy, old wood.

Dr. Cotton picked up the brandy bottle and began to pour out brandy for his guests.

"Mrs. Coyne?" said Melanie Cotton. "Will you take coffee?" Mrs. Coyne would. "Cream and sugar?" Mrs. Coyne, an ample woman already, took two spoons of sugar and cream.

"Dr. DeGraaf," said Cotton, "you've been very silent for a while. Did my advocacy of death upset you?"

Cotton handed DeGraaf a snifter of brandy.

"I'm afraid not, Dr. Cotton. Actually, I was feeling too contented to talk. Lovely dinner. Beautiful house."

"Ah. Thank you."

"The head over the fireplace—is it a grizzly or a brown?"

"Brown. Some of them have that tannish flecking. Taxidermy is a hobby of mine."

"I wasn't evading your question, though. Actually I wish your views did upset me."

"You wish they did? Why is that, sir?"

"Dr. Cotton, you say you're in favor of doing away with the hopelessly ill rather than keeping them alive by extraordinary treatment. Well, I wish it was the sort of world where such an idea was shocking. A world, for instance, where we had plenty of equipment, ample nursing staffs, and everything we needed to take care of everybody who needed it. But it isn't like that. So we make hard decisions all the time, and about most of them we aren't in the least upset."

"So you're one of us, then? You're in favor of pulling the plug on a patient who's hopelessly brain damaged?"

"Not necessarily. I don't see any problem in keeping the patient alive if it doesn't hurt anyone else. I'm just arguing that we should be honest with ourselves. If there's one respirator and twenty patients who need it, and we decide not to remove the hopeless patient who is using it, we're certainly denying use of it to the other nineteen. And that's not very different from pulling the plug on *them*."

Cotton ducked his head with its sharp little nose, then pulled it back up. He did not, DeGraaf thought, enjoy being disagreed with. He had thin fingers with knobby joints clutched around his drink, hands like talons, and he made comments by pecking forward with his head, the movements of a carnivorous bird.

Melanie Cotton had overheard, and said, "That's exactly my point, Dr. DeGraaf. We're making hard decisions, but we have to make them case by case. We can't just have a policy to unplug any patient who reaches a given condition."

"Can't we, my dear?" said her father. "Why not?"

"It's too mechanical. It doesn't take into consideration the equipment available or the needs of the patient or his family."

"The needs of a patient who will never, ever again, be conscious?" her father asked.

"Yes, even that patient."

"That's meaningless. And as to a uniform policy being too mechanical, that's exactly why we should have policies. They act to prevent whim and unpredictable behavior. They result," said Adam Cotton, pouncing with his head, "in that very elusive attribute in human events—fairness."

There was a silence. Most of the people in the room had stopped to listen to the discussion. Now there was a strained silence. The subject was a serious one, certainly, but the father and the daughter had been speaking with far more seriousness than is usual in after-dinner conversation. No one quite wanted to agree with either person, for fear of offending the other.

Then Cotton's sister, Helen Spruance, gasped:

"But you can't actually mean that decent doctors let people die!"

And her nephew blurted, "Good God, Aunt Helen, where have you *been?*"

Everyone laughed and the moment passed.

But not the underlying tension.

Now, DeGraaf has never claimed to be prescient. He admits he did not feel any storm approaching ready to sweep up himself and the others. But he did notice cross-currents of emotion that seemed to him excessive for the place and time. In addition, he did not feel that all the tension came from the family. He found the situation rather interesting. He swirled his brandy, wriggled his back comfortably nearer the fire, and watched

For a few moments he studied Mrs. Spruance. The family leanness that in Adam Cotton's case looked like sharpness in Helen Spruance's case became fragility. Her face, too, had none of his pointed intelligence. She had cottony white hair and wore a fluffy chiffon dress in a lilac shade. She waved her little hands helplessly, saying, "After all, I don't think it's a nice topic. You people always insist on talking about things like that at dinner. Mrs. Coyne, let's think of something else."

"But Uncle Adam is absolutely right, Aunt Helen," said her nephew. "It's a waste of money and everybody's talent to keep useless people alive. You'd think with millions of people starving—"

"*Please*, Alec," said his aunt.

"Yes, Alec, please," said Adam Cotton nastily. "When you start advocating my view, it makes me begin to doubt whether I'm right."

The young man turned red.

Rather than watch an unpleasant family scene, DeGraaf stared around the room. His eye fell on another young man, Dr. Passim, from Saudi Arabia. Already a physician, he was in the United States studying a graduate specialty. DeGraaf had seen him around the hospital cafeteria. Now Passim was bending toward Melanie Cotton, saying, "Black, no sugar, thank you."

"I thought," said Melanie, "that Arabian coffee was always made very sweet."

"Aha. Yes," said Passim. "But not all those in the United States like the hot dog, either. Yes?"

"Yes," she said. She gave him his coffee, her square, competent hands looking strangely graceful. Her nails were blunt-cut to make it easier to scrub several times a day and to fit into rubber gloves. In her case, it suited her style. She was a compact, eager, efficient girl, DeGraaf thought, quite different from her acerbic, stringy father. She smiled warmly at Passim and he glowed. Perhaps he was finding this cold country difficult.

"Peter!" she called. "Tell Dr. Passim about the time you were a student and knocked off a whole tray of instruments on the state supervisor's foot."

"Well, that's almost the whole story already," said an unusually handsome man of about thirty-five. But he came over and picked up the cue. Passim, he probably realized, had made errors at work that had embarrassed him. Peter led him to a pair of folding chairs, sat, and in a few seconds had the man laughing.

Melanie noticed DeGraaf watching. "Dr. Passim is very sensitive," she said.

"He's working with your father, isn't he?"

Her face sobered. "Yes. I realize Dad can be difficult—" She reached for two more cups. "Dad? Dr. Coyne? More coffee?" The two were standing nearer the fire.

"No, thank you, dear," said Coyne, loudly and heartily. "Got brandy."

Cotton merely swirled his glass of brandy and said, "Melanie, don't interrupt."

She had begun pouring and now stared down at the half-filled cup. How often, DeGraaf wondered, did this young woman have to cover up for her father's rudeness?

DeGraaf said, "Don't stop. I'll take a whole cup. I'm a coffee freak."

"So am I," she said. She filled the rest of the half-full one and then poured a second for herself. As she smiled up at him, DeGraaf thought she looked like an elf with freckles.

Rather breathlessly, she said, "I find it awfully hard to talk with people I've had as teachers, like you, Dr. DeGraaf. I always feel as if—if I'm being polite, I'm just trying to butter them up for an A in the class. Which is pretty silly, considering I haven't been in classes for a long time."

"It would help if you called me Gerritt," he said, and she giggled nicely. "I think I know everybody here except the young man who calls your father Uncle Adam. Who is he?"

"Oh, weren't you introduced? That was sloppy of us." She stopped, as if the last remark sounded too slick to her. "Actually, we don't have that many parties." There was a need for honesty in this girl, DeGraaf thought, that was unusual and charming. "He's Alec Spruance, Aunt Helen's nephew, really. Aunt Helen is a widow and he is her husband's brother's son."

"Does he live here, too?"

"Lord, no! Oh, dear." She put her hand to her face. "I shouldn't sound so pleased about it. But it would be *impossible* around here if he did. He's at Pengill's Prep right now. His parents are dead. He's seventeen and he's going through the absolutely-positive stage. And my father—"

"Yes?"

"I guess father never outgrew that stage."

"I see."

"Alec will graduate in June, two months from now. And then we're going to send him on a trip before he leaves for college."

"Now, Peter Erikson I know. Mostly from running into him in the hospital cafeteria. Didn't I hear that you two were engaged?"

"Yes, we are." And she did that incredible thing that took her back to her early teens instead of her early thirties. She blushed.

DeGraaf, speaking of Erikson, turned to glance at him and Passim, and he saw Passim staring fixedly over Erikson's shoulder at Adam Cotton. The look on his face was one of hopeless fear.

Cotton did not notice. He clapped his hands sharply and said, "Well! I've set out some cards for you."

"All by yourself, Adam?" drawled Dr. Coyne.

"No, not exactly. I write out the hands. My good Mrs. Johns does the actual sorting and making up. She's put them over on the window seat, all neatly labelled and packaged in rubber bands."

"And just how will you play, since you know what devious surprises you've made up?"

"I don't play. Surely you see there are eight of you. Two tables exactly. In any case I have work to do. I'm in the middle of revising an article. Going to show the medical implications of the deaths of one Jimmy Wigoda and one Aileen Lee. I'll sit by the fire and spin while you people play. Helen, didn't you have the gardener set out any extra firewood?"

"Why, yes, Adam. It's right there."

"This isn't right, Helen. There are hardly any large pieces. It's almost all kindling. The fire's already started. We don't need kindling."

"I didn't know. Shall I go find some right now?"

"No, but for heaven's sake, Helen! All you have to do is supervise the help. Do you think that's too much for you?"

"Not at all, Adam," she said nervously. Her hands fluttered around her neck.

"Do you play bridge, Dr. Passim?" Erikson asked, loudly and firmly.

"Oh, most assuredly, most assuredly," said

Passim, stepping farther away from Adam Cotton.

"What if I don't want to play?" asked young Alec.

"You want to," said Cotton, sitting in his chair, and adjusting it to face the fire at an angle. The coffee table with his manuscript stood directly in front of the blaze. The wing chair Cotton had selected turned diagonally away from them. A heavy chair, upholstered in dark green wool, its high back and side wings effectively closed Cotton away from the rest of the company. On the table near his hand was his glass of brandy. Simply by sitting down he had gotten rid of them.

"Dismissed, b'gad," said Dr. Peter Erikson, cheerfully.

Dr. Coyne strolled over to the drinks table. "Whiskey, soda, rum, gin, tonic, brandy, and plenty of ice. I can very easily stand *that* sort of dismissal." Mrs. Coyne followed, watching him. He poured himself a whiskey and soda with a defiant air and walked with it toward the two card tables.

Melanie smiled determinedly at the group. "They've laid out six games," she said. "Either Dad assumes that's all we'll want to play, or we only own twelve decks. Of course, we can always go on playing after we finish the duplicates."

"Good," said Peter. "Where do you want us?"

"Well, let's split couples. We usually do. Dad says there's no intrafamily warfare that way. That would mean one of the Coynes at each table, and you and I should separate, Peter. And everyone— just pick a chair."

The folding chairs had been grouped around the room to provide conversation spots for the coffee and brandy period. Now each player picked one up and carried it to the card tables.

"Be my partner, Passim?" said Peter Erikson.

"Thank you," said Passim, evidently delighted to be asked.

"How about you, Dr. DeGraaf?" said Mrs. Coyne. DeGraaf smiled and nodded.

"And I'll take you, Alec," said Melanie. "All right?"

"If you insist," said the nephew, with poor grace. Melanie moved her chair to the table. DeGraaf suspected her of trying to avoid inflicting her sour young relative on anyone else. He took up a position next to Melanie on her left, with his back to the distant fire. The tables were so far from the blaze that he would feel only the slightest warmth, but he did not like looking into lights when he was playing cards. And even the slight warmth would be pleasant.

At the other table Dr. Coyne had taken Aunt Helen as partner against Dr. Passim and Dr. Erikson, so all was well. Melanie brought over her table's first pile of cards, carefully labelled "first hand" and separated into north, south, east and west.

"The windows face north," Melanie said. They distributed, then looked at their cards.

At this point DeGraaf stopped talking and pulled over a pencil. He glanced at me, then scribbled on the white bar top. "We sat in these positions. Of course, you *knew* all this," he added argumentatively.

He was right. I did. He produced a sketch of the library with the positions of all the people there, as they had been during the bridge game:

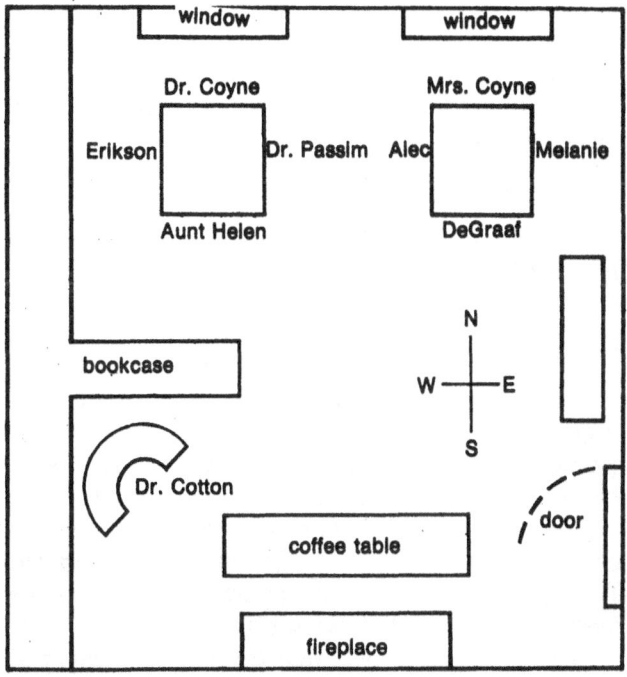

Mrs. Coyne, DeGraaf went on, had bid one heart. Melanie passed; DeGraaf bid two hearts and Alec bid two spades. DeGraaf suspected that Alec's bid was unwise, since his own hand also held good spades. No doubt Melanie knew from experience how her partner played. In any case, Mrs. Coyne went to game, taking the bidding.

They tried not to hear the bidding at the next table, and once they were into the play, they did not notice. DeGraaf was dummy. He spread a hand that was only adequate, but Mrs. Coyne said, "Good," in a tone that made it clear she was approving his bidding, not his cards.

He sat enjoying watching the people. This was the privilege of being dummy. It was interesting in itself to see the way people's characters came out in play. A game like this was a socially approved form of aggression. Areas of behavior that would not be noticeable in cocktail party conversation appeared, completely unguarded here. Mrs. Coyne, for instance, a cautious conversationalist, played like a riverboat gambler, which is to say she never gambled, but assessed the opposition shrewdly and played quickly, decisively, and well.

At the next table Dr. Coyne sat in the north chair. He appeared to be having a harder time of the hand than his wife. Certainly, DeGraaf thought, he would not have been impulsive enough to go beyond game? He licked his upper lip, hesitated, studied the cards again before leading. He offered a card, as if for slaughter. The previously mild Dr. Passim said "Hah!" and apparently trumped the lead. Erikson nodded pleasantly.

DeGraaf looked at Helen Spruance, dummy at that table, her face blank and somehow out of focus, oblivious to the game.

"Made it," said Mrs. Coyne, recalling him to his table.

"We'll get you next time," Melanie said cheerfully.

But they did not. DeGraaf took one look at his cards and said, "Three no trump."

Alec groaned. "Uncle Adam's just doing this to me," he said.

"Alec, don't be silly," said Melanie. "Daddy didn't know where you were going to sit."

"All right. All right. But he would if he could."

DeGraaf watched Alec lead. A king of diamonds. Melanie sighed. Conventional wisdom would have told Alec to lead the fourth from the highest card in his best suit, both to give his partner a chance to decide whether to take the trick or not after she had seen the board, and to cue her as to which suit he was strong in, so that she could lead it later. Mrs. Coyne put her hand to her mouth to hide her expression. The long red fingernails across her lips made her look like a shark. She said, "Well . . ." and laid out her hand. In it was the ace of diamonds.

The hand was not difficult to play, but DeGraaf found it fun. Mrs. Coyne got up and silently walked around behind him to study his hand, said nothing, and, satisfied, moved off. She circled the other table as well, visited the drink table, and returned in time to see DeGraaf make his bid with one overtrick. She was very self-contained, very controlled. De-Graaf wondered why she needed to be.

By now Alec was annoyed. He tore the rubber band off his next hand, looked at the cards with a sneer, and then DeGraaf saw a secretive look come into the boy's eyes.

The bidding went as Alec's behavior had led De-Graaf to expect. Melanie had bid diamonds. Alec changed to hearts and inexorably raised to game. Four hearts. Melanie studied the boy at each bid, evidently doubtful that he could make it. She gave the minimum required response. But he paid no attention to the weakness of her answers. As they took the bid, Mrs. Coyne doubled. Melanie bit her lip.

Mrs. Coyne led directly into DeGraaf's best suit, clubs. Melanie laid out a dummy that contained low clubs and DeGraaf took the trick. Sighing, Melanie got up and went to get coffee. She poured some for DeGraaf, took the shake of Mrs. Coyne's head to mean "No" and poured some for her aunt.

She took the coffee back and got the brandy, asking her father whether he wanted some more. He grunted and she poured an inch into his glass.

Meanwhile, Alec was meeting resistance. And he did not reveal self-reliance, only sullenness. He slapped his cards against his left hand as if they had intentionally let him down. His opponents, De-Graaf and Glynis Coyne had immediately seized three out of the first four tricks and although he picked up two after that, it was clear he would go down dismally. And doubled. DeGraaf noted with amusement that Melanie did not even glance at Alec's hand before she sat down, she must have been so certain he'd lost it. Across the room Aunt Helen had become dummy and wandered over slowly to look at the fire. By that time Alec had lost.

The fourth hand was taken in the bidding by Melanie—fortunately, since it gave Alec a chance to be dummy and go stamping around the room instead of sitting at the table glowering. They could hear him clattering glasses on the beverage table just as noisily as possible without breaking them. Melanie glanced his way and shook her head. But she played efficiently, squeaking through, and got the first score her side had won. Alec returned and looked at the tricks laid out in front of Melanie.

"You were lucky," he said ungraciously.

Alec bid an equally difficult five diamonds on the next hand. DeGraaf happened to be sitting in the last seat permitted to double at the end of the bidding. He knew he ought to double, but he was genuinely reluctant to do it, in view of what Melanie had had to put up with. For a moment he thought of going to an impossible, higher bid himself to help her out, to keep her from losing so severely. But a glance at Mrs. Coyne stopped him. It was her bland confidence that he would do the correct thing. He could not let his partner down.

"Double," he said.

Alec looked at him sourly. Melanie seemed to be repressing a smile, her lips pressed together.

It went as expected. Indeed it was so clearly a walkover that DeGraaf found himself staring around the room for long periods while Alec studied a feeble hand desperately for inspiration that never came. Coyne, on the other side of the room, paced around a couple of minutes, wiping his face with a handkerchief. Next DeGraaf heard the clink of bottles and stoppers. Melanie, seeing Coyne pouring a drink, got up to ask him whether the ice was fresh or starting to melt.

"Nope, nice and hard. That's a very decent ice bucket," Coyne said in his loud, hearty voice.

It was DeGraaf's lead. He no sooner dropped the card, spinning, on the table, when Alec slammed down his hand in a fury and said, "All right! All right! The rest are yours." He leaned back and crossed his arms. Mrs. Coyne unemotionally inscribed the score. They had gone down three doubled.

"I quit!" said Alec.

"Oh, Alec, you can't!" Melanie gasped.

"Yes I can."

"But then you'll spoil the game for everybody."

"So what? It won't hurt them. They've won."

"But Alec, the point of duplicate bridge is to see which team does better with the same cards. Dr. DeGraaf and Mrs. Coyne may have had better cards than we have. But we're not really playing them. We're playing against Peter and Dr. Passim at the other table who have the same cards we have. That's what's nice about it. It eliminates luck."

"And you may beat them," said DeGraaf.

"It could be that east-west is set up to go down. But if *we* go down less than *they* do, we win," said Melanie.

"And no reason why you shouldn't," DeGraaf added. "You're a natural player. You've got all the equipment."

As he waited for the thunderbolt that strikes liars, DeGraaf reflected on Alec's equipment for cards. Two hands and two eyes were about the extent of it, as far as he could see. Then a bright thought struck him. If by "natural player" he could have meant uneducated and unreflective, then he was not even a liar.

"Oh, hell," said Alec. "I guess it isn't fair to let the rest of you down."

Mrs. Coyne cast her clear eyes around the table and calmly handed out the next packs of cards.

They played the last hand, Mrs. Coyne easily raking in a four spades bid. Alec was silent.

"That's the last of the hands Daddy made up," Melanie said. "How about another couple of hands of our own?"

"I'm game," said Mrs. Coyne.

"What's the difference?" said Alec. They took this as agreement.

"Peter!" Melanie called.

"Yes?"

"We'll put aside our score and compare later, okay? We're going to do a few more hands."

"Sure, dear. We're just finishing the last."

"Shall we also play another after?" asked Passim. "I find this much fun and your company so pleasant."

"Sure thing," said Peter.

Three more hands merely established DeGraaf's and Mrs. Coyne's dominance at their table. The lady showed no inclination whatever to let Alec and Melanie win a hand, in spite of an illegal eyebrow-raising DeGraaf directed at her once when the cards broke in Alec's favor. They swept on to game, a smashing victory that left Alec white and sullen and even Melanie a little subdued.

At the other table, Dr. Coyne yawned.

He said, "Sorry." Then he called over to his wife, "Don't you think we ought to call it a night?"

"If you say so, darling," said his wife complacently.

"How did your table do?" Melanie asked.

The other table, it turned out, had pretty much split the difference. In fact they had gone the six duplicate hands without anybody making game, though both teams had scores above and below the line. This left DeGraaf and Mrs. Coyne the clear winners of the evening.

"How about a nightcap?" Melanie asked. Peter came over to her and put an arm around her waist. Dr. Coyne said,

"No, I'd better not. I have surgery first thing tomorrow. "Hope your father's got his work done, though. We certainly gave him time."

"A lovely evening," said Mrs. Coyne.

Dr. Coyne called, "Adam! We're going to leave. Thanks for the party." There was no answer. He walked closer to make sure he was heard.

"Shall we put another log on the fire?" Melanie asked Peter, "or do you think it's too late?"

"Let's put one on and sit up a while."

"Melanie," Dr. Coyne said in a suddenly quieter voice, "I think you should come here a minute."

There was a silence. Melanie walked quickly to Coyne and the only sounds in the room were her footsteps and a piece of burned wood falling in the hearth.

Then Melanie said, "Oh," and stood near Dr. Coyne, looking at her father as if something hurt her. Peter went over immediately.

DeGraaf also crossed to them. Dr. Adam Cotton still sat in his chair facing the fire. He was leaning into the big winged back. Nearly hidden by the right wing, where his temple leaned into the chair, the handle of a small silvery knife protruded from his head. Coyne had not touched the body, nor did DeGraaf, but he looked closely for a moment, as Aunt Helen began to moan somewhere in the background.

Even knowing it was there, it was difficult to see the knife handle, with the head turned into the corner of the chair. But it was evident to DeGraaf that the blade had been driven in through the temple, where the parietal bone was extremely thin. If the blade was longer than an inch or so, it would have severed so many connections in the brain that any response by Cotton would have been impossible. He would not likely have made a sound.

DeGraaf said, "Would you mind, Melanie, if I gave some instructions?"

She was trembling when he looked at her, but she had her voice under control. "No. No, go ahead. I'll just sit down."

Aunt Helen was beginning to make gulping noises. Mrs. Coyne seized her by the shoulders and walked her firmly toward the table full of drinks.

DeGraaf said: "Coyne, would you go to the phone in the hall and dial 388-7575? Just explain what's happened and ask them to send Craddock if they can. Peter, will you go check what servants are in the house and tell them not to leave? Will everyone else please sit down somewhere. I'll stand here while we wait."

# CHAPTER TWO

That was where I came in. I didn't know who had called but I knew the desk had sent the team ahead before they had called me at home, forcing me to put on my shoes and the tie I had tossed happily over the blender when I had come in the back door at ten after six. It was eleven-thirty and no telling when I'd get to bed.

The team had arrived there ahead of me, of course. When I walked in the uniformed man announced, "Here's Inspector Craddock," and I heard somebody say, "Rob! Good!" It was DeGraaf, so I knew who had gotten me out of my warm house.

"Splendid!" I said. "This makes it easy for us. Who did it?"

"I am desolated to say I wasn't watching."

"My luck is holding, I see. All right. Let's get the technicalities over."

"It looks to me as if they're nearly over now," DeGraaf said, nodding toward the officer with the photographic equipment, who was standing with his hands on his hips. The man from the ME's office was sitting in a chair. "If he's got all his pictures, you can start," I said. I looked at the officer and he nodded. "I want photographs of the rest of the room too, just in case." At the same moment the men from the morgue arrived, and I told them to wait until the ME's man had finished. Then I started off the fingerprint man, Lonnie, who was new and hadn't wanted to breathe until I told him where and how. At the same time I was scanning the room.

"You tell me, Gerritt, how somebody could stab a man in the head, in the same room with you, and you miss the whole thing. Jeez!"

"We were playing cards. Rob, look at this place. The two card tables are set up under the windows of the north wall. The fireplace and the coffee table in front of it and Cotton's chair to one side of that are near the south wall. It's a long room, thirty to thirty-five feet. And between Cotton's chair and the card tables are two things: a table with refreshments against the east wall and a bookcase jutting out at right angles from the west wall. At my table maybe three people could see the back of Cotton's chair— Melanie, Alec, and Mrs. Coyne. I could have only if I had turned around; my back was to that end of the room. At the other card table, most of them couldn't see Cotton's chair because of the bookcase. On top of *that*, the back of Cotton's chair was so high that you could look right at it without seeing Cotton himself."

"All right, all right. I can understand that much, but the fact is you were all here keeping your eyes on each other." Just then the morgue men shoved the hamper up next to Cotton's body and started to lift him in. The knife had been removed from his head and only a trickle of blood, mostly dry, running down next to his eye gave any indication of what had happened to him. The body made a dry, rustling sound as they lowered it into the hamper and closed the lid.

Lonnie held the knife gently on a piece of tissue.

"I want that left here," I said. "Try for latents here and now and photograph it in detail. Not that there's any chance of somebody being stupid enough to handle it barehanded—"

"It's covered with prints, sir," said Lonnie.

"Oh? Maybe we're gonna get lucky. Well, go ahead." I turned to DeGraaf. "What were we saying?"

"*You* said we were all keeping our eyes on each other. But we weren't. We were playing bridge."

"What of it? You were all sitting with cards in your hands, weren't you? I don't play bridge, but when I play poker I watch people for sure."

"Not bridge. In each hand one person's set of cards is laid down and played from the board by the bidder. Then the person whose hand is laid down is dummy."

"Dummy. So what?"

"So he doesn't play. He can get up and wander around the room as much as he wants and no one thinks twice about it."

"Oh, hell."

"Exactly. And in this room—" he paced around over to the card table, back to the table full of glasses and bottles, back to the fire. "You get up from the game, saunter over to fill up your drink. Maybe stroll over here to watch the fire burn. Say, look at this."

"What?"

"If I stand here, behind the coffee table, looking at the fire, I'll bet I still couldn't tell that Cotton was dead. Rob, will you sit in Cotton's chair a minute?"

"Anything to help."

"Now look at this. No, back farther, with your head leaning into the angle where the wing meets the back, at your right side. Good. I think that's just how he was. Now I stand behind the coffee table looking towards the fire in a normal, guest-like position. If I turn and look at you, I see your legs, part of your lap, your left hand and just a little bit of your face, turned away from me. That's all." He glanced down at the coffee table and the papers on it. "We'd better save those, you know."

"I am already aware of that. We don't usually walk onto a murder scene and immediately start throwing things out."

"And the bridge scores," he went on, blandly. "At very least, they'll tell us who was dummy when."

"Naturally—"

"No, don't get up, Rob. I'm not through with this."

"Mmmf."

"Go back to Cotton's position. I'm going to walk between the coffee table and the fire. Probably no one did this. It's too hot, for one thing. But even so, all I see is the whole of your left side and some of the right arm. But I don't see the right side of your head, with the scalpel in it—"

"Scalpel?"

"Sure. Didn't you see it?"

"Of course I saw it. I didn't know what it was. So one of these respectable doctor types did it, huh?"

"Maybe. One of these doctor types is the victim. So maybe one is the murderer also."

"Sure," I said, getting up.

"No, stay there a minute more. Now how can I get into a position to see the knife? I can walk directly between you and the fire. That isn't very polite and no guest would just do it casually. Or I can walk all the way around behind you, here, between you and the bookcases and come up to you on your right side. That also would not be a thing a guest would do casually."

"So what are we bothering for? I've got people to interview."

"Good lord, Rob. Do you always just plunge in feet first? You're going to be trying to decide which witnesses are telling you things that could be true. That at least."

"So?"

"We've established two things. One, that the people playing cards over there would not necessarily see what was going on over here. In other words, if somebody says he didn't see anything, he may be perfectly trustworthy."

"Wonderful."

"And second, anyone may have come to this end of the room, even as far as to stand near the fire, and not have seen that Cotton was dead."

"Well, for proving two negatives which tell me nothing, that's great."

"Don't be silly. You need the ground clear. For instance, you might have concluded that if a guest came and stood near the fire at ten o'clock and did not notice that Cotton was dead, then he had not been stabbed by that time. If you had thought that, you could completely mess up your idea about the time of death."

"Oh, all right. I give you that. But after all, wouldn't anybody notice that he wasn't breathing? I mean, half of these people are doctors and doctors know enough to expect people to breathe."

"I don't know. Lie back again and let me look."

"Okay. Here."

"Oh. Well, we've got a problem with that, too. The light from the fire casts moving shadows on your body. You'd have to be looking especially to see whether he was breathing to notice that he wasn't."

"Damn. Still, if anyone spoke to him and he didn't answer, that would be conclusive."

"Afraid not."

"Oh, come on! Damn it Gerritt! You just enjoy making things difficult."

"No I'm not. Not with Adam Cotton. If somebody spoke to Adam Cotton and he didn't answer, they'd think a lot of things, but not necessarily that he was dead."

"That kind of a guy, huh?"

"That kind of a guy."

I had thought of holding the interviews in the library, where the murder had taken place. Sometimes with impulsive killers you can intimidate them and they'll blurt out something they meant to keep back. However, DeGraaf's interest in the library convinced me that sight lines and so on were going to be important here. I hastily sketched a plan of the library. DeGraaf described who had been sitting where. With this plan, I felt I had a chance of learning whether one of the suspects claimed to have seen too much or too little. Naturally, this kind of questioning had to be done elsewhere so that they couldn't look around the room and check on whether their lies were physically possible.

I posted a guard in the library and removed myself and DeGraaf to a smaller room called the study. A uniformed man came with us as far as the study door.

"Shall I send anyone in, sir?" he asked.

"Send in Turgid to take notes. And let's start with the ones who don't live here. We might as well let them go as soon as possible. Make certain they've been printed before they leave, though."

"Yes, sir."

"Okay. Go get me somebody."

The first somebody was the foreign doctor, Passim. He came through the door sideways, as if trying to be less visible. But he must have realized this was hopeless, for he straightened up.

DeGraaf, naturally, felt sorry for him. The young man had been plunged into a police investigation in an unfamiliar country. He couldn't know what to expect of police methods and would probably believe that he had been called first because he looked the most suspicious. I would have struck hard while he felt uncertain to see what turned up. But De-Graaf said, "May I?"

And of course I had to say, "Okay."

"Dr. Passim, you know it is necessary to ask questions of people who were present at a violent death."

"Oh, of course. Most natural."

"It doesn't suggest any particular suspicion. We are taking first the people who don't live in the house, so they can go home."

"Yes. I see. Most courteous. Such a great loss is this."

At that, DeGraaf nodded to me. I looked at him sourly. Now that the suspect had no fear of me, Gerritt would permit me to begin. I said, "Let me have your full name."

"Ibid Passim."

"And where are you from, Mr. Passim?"

"Dr. Passim, sir. I am from what you call Saudi Arabia."

"And what are you doing here?"

"I am studying a specialty that is not taught in my country."

"What specialty?"

"Vascular surgery."

"DeGraaf, what the hell is that?"

"If you need something special done to your blood vessels, you call a vascular surgeon."

"What kind of damn specialty are they going to think of next? Toenails?"

"There is such a thing already. Anyway, you wouldn't feel so funny about it if one of your main body arteries was threatening a blowout."

"No. I suppose not." I looked at Passim, who had laughed once, rather doubtfully. "You do that kind of work?"

"Oh, yes, sir. Exactly. That is why I am here."

"All right. And why were you invited tonight?"

"Why? As to that, how can I know, sir?"

"I mean, what is your connection with the people here?"

"Oh. Yes, I see." He rubbed his hands together, with a sound like sand blowing across a desert. "I was a student of Dr. Cotton. That is to say, Dr. Cotton was the head of vascular surgery. I am a graduate doctor in my home country and I come here to do additional work."

"I get it now. And while you were here tonight, what did you notice?"

"Notice? Nothing, I think."

"When you were—what the hell—dummy, did you walk around the room?"

"I don't—oh, yes. Assuredly. I went to the table and made a gin and tonic. Very nice."

"Did you see anybody? Was anybody dummy from the other table and wandering around the room at the same time?"

"Ah. Let me see. We were, I think, out of synchronization, you might say. When I was up I believe the boy was once, also. But not all of the time." "Did you see Cotton?"

"Oh, no, sir. Not at all. Not during the bridge. I did not go near him, or that side of the room."

"Did you see anybody else approach him?"

"No."

"What did you see while you were playing?"

Passim, we knew, sat in the east position at the second table, which was the only chair at that table from which Cotton's chair could be seen at all. However, had Passim noticed it, most of his view of Cotton's chair was obscured by the bookcase. He would see the fireplace and the coffee table clearly. As Passim tried to recall the evening, I wondered how observant he was, and how honest.

"While I was playing, sir, I concentrated a great deal. Not to let my partner down, you see. And I believe, but I am not certain, that I could not see Dr. Cotton from where I sat. I saw the fire, I know. Several people approached that area. I think they went to look at the fire, or to warm themselves."

"But they could have gone past the fire to Cotton's chair?"

"Oh, yes, sir. As far as I know."

"Who?"

"Who?"

"Who went to the fire?"

"Oh, yes. Dr. Coyne, I believe sir. His wife. I think—yes, I am certain—I saw Mrs. Spruance go and stand near to the fire and stay for quite some time, holding out her hands. She was perhaps, cold. It is not always that buildings here are warm enough. Dr. Cotton too."

"Dr. Cotton? He got up to look at the fire? When was that?"

"Not Dr. Cotton the father. Dr. Melanie Cotton."

"Oh." I had thought we were about to find a time that Cotton—for sure—had been alive. DeGraaf's idea that he might have been killed any time from the beginning to the end of the bridge game was upsetting. Narrowing down the time he might have been killed and finding out who could have been up and around the room then seemed my best hope. "Well, all right. Anybody else get up?"

"I believe my partner did, when he was dummy and I was playing the hand. But of that I am less certain. I am concentrating when I play the hand. I am responsible for it, you see."

"Yes, I see. That was Dr. Erikson, huh?"

"Yes. But such a nice man. He would not hurt Dr. Cotton. Such a kind man. I am sorry. It is not my business to say that."

"What about the others?"

"Um, Dr. DeGraaf, here, I did not notice near the fire. Nor the boy."

"Okay. Did you hear anything strange?"

"No."

"A scream or a moan?"

"I am sorry. No."

"All right, Dr. Passim. We'll write up what you've told us and somebody'll catch you tomorrow and have you sign it. A man's going to ask you for your fingerprints on your way out, if he hasn't already. Just routine."

"Yes, sir." Passim rose, evidently relieved. He certainly wasn't worried about fingerprints.

"Just one thing," said DeGraaf.

"Yes, sir?"

"Did you like Dr. Cotton?"

A look of alarm came to Passim's face, and as quickly vanished. With some dignity, he said,

"I do not have to like a man to respect him."

"Thank you," said DeGraaf. After Passim exited, he said, "And one up to Dr. Passim."

"I hope we're not going to get this from everybody."

"What?"

"See no evil, hear no evil."

"Well, I warned you. After all, I didn't notice anything wrong."

"Ha! That's an expert for you!"

"And really, Rob, you have to realize that if anybody, other than the killer, saw the murder taking place, he'd have raised a cry. Surely you don't expect X to walk in here and say he saw Y stab Cotton, but not wanting to interrupt his four spades bid he said nothing?"

With great forebearance, I said, "What I am hoping for is that somebody saw or heard something that *on reflection* and with knowledge that murder has taken place, becomes significant."

"Good luck."

DeGraaf, of course, likes to imagine that things will be difficult so that he will have the fun of figuring them out.

The uniformed man popped his head in the door:

"I asked Dr. Erikson to come in next, but he said he'd just as soon keep Miss Cotton—Dr. Cotton— company as go home. So, do you want Dr. and Mrs. Coyne together or separately?"

"Separately. They're separate people. And I told you to stay with the suspects. Oh, never mind. Just go get one of 'em."

Mrs. Coyne walked in unhurriedly. I couldn't tell whether she was being determinedly unhurried or was just naturally unflappable. She was a bit plumper than she should have been, and wore an absolutely straight unornamented beige sheath dress with only a gold choker. She resembled a bratwurst. She set a white bag down on the floor next to her chair and sat, without asking any nervous questions, looking right at me. This was a situation where you go for the appealing approach.

"Mrs. Coyne," I said. "You know the situation. Can you help us in any way? Can you tell us what you saw and heard during the evening?"

"Of course, up to a point. Naturally, I've been thinking about that, ever since the discovery of the —of Dr. Cotton. But I really mostly saw things like clubs and hearts and so on."

"Still—"

"I was about to say that I'm aware that I was facing the end of the room where Dr. Cotton was sitting. In fact Melanie Cotton and I surely had, between us, the best view of that end of the room of anyone. Melanie's was more diagonal, and therefore, though she might have been able to see more of her father's chair, she might have been looking that way less often."

"That's very true."

"I'm trying extremely hard, Inspector Craddock, not to say hastily that I didn't see anything unusual. The reason I say hastily is that I wasn't paying attention at all to the other side of the room. But probably one can't help noticing things subconsciously. I can tell you more or less who got up to stretch or get drinks. Everyone at the other table did, most of them more than once. At our table only Dr. DeGraaf didn't get up at all."

"Where did these people go, to the best of your recollection?"

"Either to the beverage table or to look at the fire. My husband went to look at the fire once and to get a drink once. Mrs. Spruance went to the fire. She stood there for quite a while. I believe all the others did as well, except Dr. DeGraaf. And—oh—I believe Alec Spruance never went to the fireplace. I watched him a little because he was so angry."

"Angry?"

"He is a very bad bridge player. Any kind of game, I should think, not just cards, because his problem is not a basic inability, but a tendency to get very emotional about it. Then, of course, he can't think at all. He bids according to whether he thinks it's about time for him to make a big killing, rather than on the basis of the cards he has drawn."

"Would you say you knew exactly what his movements were?" Let me, I thought, eliminate *somebody*.

"No, I certainly could not. As I say, I pay attention when I play cards. If there were a difficult lead coming up, he could have stood on his head in the other end of the room and I wouldn't have noticed."

"All right. What about you? Did you go into the far part of the room?"

"Yes. I remember getting up while Dr. DeGraaf was playing a three no trump. I think that must have been the second hand. I walked around and looked at his cards. There was no doubt that if he played them correctly he would make the bid and I was very confident that he would play them well. So I went and got a drink."

"Nothing else?"

"I may have walked around a few minutes. I can't think of anything important."

DeGraaf said, "Mrs. Coyne, did you know Adam Cotton well?"

"I wouldn't say well at all. Cotton wasn't a clubby sort. My husband is eight or ten years younger than Adam Cotton is. Was. They were in the same specialty, so they ran into each other constantly at the hospital. But I hardly ever saw him."

"You've been at his house before, though?"

"No, never."

"Really? Tonight was the first time you'd been here? Your husband too?"

"Yes. We had Dr. Cotton to dinner once at our house. I've heard from some of the other men's wives that Cotton would have a party like this about once every six months. He'd invite some of his family, as you see, and two or three people from the hospital. He'd worked his way down, over the last few years, through the older men, I guess, so maybe it was simply our turn."

"Were his parties always for bridge, like this?"

"So I've heard."

"Mrs. Coyne, what can you tell us about him as a person?"

"I hardly know. He was said to be something of a miser. And he wasn't a—oh, I don't know how to say this. He wasn't an especially pleasant person. Students and residents were always afraid of him. He was domineering. All this is just gossip, not personal knowledge, you know, Dr. DeGraaf."

She had said it. DeGraaf gets on tangents like this. I brought the conversation back to the point. "Did you hear anything tonight like a cry or moan?"

"No. That's strange, isn't it?"

"Maybe so. Nothing else you can tell us? Well, I'll let you go. We'll see your husband next, and then you can get home. Unless Dr. DeGraaf has another question?"

"None whatever. Thanks, Mrs. Coyne."

She left, stately and unhurried.

"What do you think of her?" I asked.

"She looks to me like a person who isn't sure she has enough trumps but just ran an iffy finesse past us."

"What's that supposed to mean?"

"Only that I get the impression that she's being awfully careful. And why should she be? They've been asked to dinner. An unfortunate event has occurred that is a bit awkward socially. Why should she be watching every word?"

"Maybe she always watches every word. Some people are naturally cautious."

"I would say she's naturally accurate. But that doesn't mean necessarily cautious."

"Oh, well, this isn't getting us anywhere. Let's

have the rest of the suspects. I suppose they are the only suspects? Could anybody have come in by the door while you were playing?"

"As far as I know? I think the door creaks and I think I would have noticed. More than that, I think the players facing that way would have seen somebody enter. A lot of them had a good view of the door."

"You mean the door was closed?"

"Oh, yes. The butler closed it when he left. Adam asked him to. Probably when that door is left open it causes a draft across the front of the fireplace and pulls smoke out. A door that close to a fireplace often does."

"All right. Before we go any farther, let's go check it out."

If we could be sure only the people inside the room had any chance of being involved, it would put us a step ahead. We hurried down the hall. A moose head looked disdainfully down at us. Getting used to the zoo on the walls was difficult.

The door to the library was three-quarters open, and a man inside was still going over the surfaces for prints. I took hold of the handle and pulled. This gave me a staccato creak. I closed it all the way and then pushed it open. A metallic whine, followed by bursts of creaking.

"Not loud, but loud enough, I think," DeGraaf said.

I turned to go back to the study and jumped. The uniformed man had crept up behind me.

"What do you want?"

"Well, we were taking the butler's fingerprints, sir. And he has something to say I think you ought to hear."

"I told you we'd see him last."

"I thought, sir, you might want to hear it before you interview the others."

"Oh, all right. Go get him."


"I don't want you to think I was ignoring my duties," said Johns, the butler. "Mrs. Johns was doing the dishes and glassware, and though I usually help her polish the glassware, I don't always. And Miss Melanie specifically said I could take some time off while they were playing bridge because the beverages were all set out and the ice and glasses. And of course I would have to be available later to help the guests on with their coats. And it wouldn't do to keep going in and out of the library, because opening the door makes the fire smoke."

"And so?" I said.

"Well, they could easily ring if they wanted more ice or glasses or water, you understand. So it wasn't as if there was anything I was supposed to be doing."

"I *see* that," I sighed.

"Then when Bart came in so upset, I happened to be in the vestibule wiping up the water the guests had tracked in. It's better to do that when they can't see you, because otherwise it might make them feel guilty."

"Yes."

"And so we sat down right there, on the bench. The one people sit on to take off their rubbers or galoshes. He was very distressed, sir. You see, Dr. Cotton had fired him this afternoon."

"Oh. Really. This person Bart?"

"Yes, sir. Dr. Cotton had said that he should put in the tulips thickly. He told him that last fall, I mean. And here it is April; they've come up. They weren't thick enough. And he fired him."

"Bart—what's his last name?"

"Pryczyk, sir."

"Go on. He was angry, was he?"

"Oh, yes, sir. Well, I felt sorry for him, you see. He just got married a little while back, a few months, and now there's a baby coming and—I just felt sorry for him."

"Sure. Is that all?"

"Oh, no, sir!" Johns looked appalled.

"All right, then what?"

"We sat down right there on the bench and talked. I was trying to suggest some other jobs he could apply for, you know. I even told him I would give him a personal recommendation. As butler I have some authority over employees and a prospective employer would know that."

"Yes, yes."

"And the point is, we sat there all evening."

"You alibi this person, Bart?"

"No, sir. I mean, yes, I suppose so, sir. But my purpose in telling you was, as you must have observed," here he paused and had the gall to look doubtful, "the bench next to the vestibule commands a view of the entire hall. We could see this door every minute. And I thought you would like to know that nobody went in."

"*What!*"

"Yes, sir."

"All evening?"

"Yes, sir."

That was it! Splendid! I could confine myself to the people inside that library. I said, "Nobody went in—including you and Bart?"

"Absolutely, sir. Nobody at all. Or came out." He got that doubtful look again, and added. "I hope I haven't taken up your time for nothing, sir. But I thought about Dr. Cotton always sitting at one end of the room. And the bridge tables are at the other end of the room. I thought if the players were very much engrossed, and I'm told people become that way about cards, they might not be certain whether anyone had entered. Then you might think an outsider did it. Which, you see, sir, one did not."

"I do see that, Mr. Johns. And I thank you. I'll talk with Mr. Pryczyk, too, of course. Later. You've been very helpful."

"Thank you, sir. I would like to have the person apprehended. Dr. Cotton may not have been an easy man to please. But I have been here for eighteen years and I have become accustomed to him."

"Thank you. On your way out, will you ask the sergeant to send in Dr. Coyne."

"Certainly, sir."

With the door closed, I turned to DeGraaf and raised my eyebrows.

DeGraaf said, "I think he was actually fond of the old sinner."

"People can probably become fond of a bunion, once they've got their shoes cut to fit. Cotton must have kept him working every waking hour. Look how he explains and explains that he wasn't really taking time off."

"He's a craftsman in his way, too, though."

"I'll tell you what we're going to do now, and this means you, not just me."

"Of course, Rob."

"We don't mention this to anyone. The others are still shut up in the dining room. If John's story holds up—and I can't imagine him telling it if it wouldn't—*and* if one of these other people tries to tell us he saw a stranger come into the room, then—" I swatted the table, hard, with the palm of my hand "—we've got him!"

"All right. There's nothing wrong with that as a strategy. I'm not optimistic about the result."

"Why not?"

"Any man or woman who has the guts to stab a man in a room full of people, assessing where everyone is, whether their minds are occupied, what the angles of sight are, plus doing it so quickly that the victim can't cry out, is not the kind of person who is going to walk into a trap."

"You never know."

"Of course you never know. That's why I say there's nothing wrong with it as a strategy. I just don't think it'll work."

"Say, do you want to go out and encourage the enemy instead of me?"

"Oh, no. I'd rather spend my time with you."

# CHAPTER THREE

Dr. Coyne was hearty, red of face, with a nose like a pink sponge, and given to nubby suits. He made no great pretense of grief at Cotton's death, and gave considerable evidence of having refreshed himself while he waited.

"Cotton's a loss to the profession, that's for sure," he said cheerfully. "But he was the most cantankerous old bastard you ever saw. All the same he was a real genius at his job."

"Respected but not liked?" DeGraaf asked mildly.

"You've hit it!" Coyne said, as if that were a particularly intelligent formulation.

I said, "I guess you and Cotton were in the same field."

"Yes, we were. He was chief of the department. Had been for years and years."

"Do you mean that people resented that? Or that you did?"

"No. It's not a job everybody wants. I wouldn't.

There are administrative details and it wouldn't suit my temperament to keep up with them. Adam enjoyed administration. Can't imagine why. But it fitted his personality."

"Which was what?"

"Oh, he liked to manage things. Never make mistakes—that was his attitude. And make sure no one else did."

"If you don't mind me saying so, that sounds like an excellent motto for a doctor."

"No doubt. That's the way the public feels. Outraged if everything isn't perfect. It's a pity, in a way. I wonder how many doctors would be practicing now if every one who ever made a mistake was thrown out. I don't imagine that anyone would be left. Except Adam Cotton, of course."

"Oh, if you put it that way—"

"You're going to say everybody's human. Sure. Easy to say when you put it in the abstract like that. But let somebody show you an actual case, with real people, where the doctor made a mistake, and you'd yell bloody murder along with the rest of them. That's the whole problem. Do you know what the rate of nervous breakdown among physicians is?"

"I can't say—"

"And Cotton did it to his students in spades! He was *unmerciful!* Most of 'em were paralyzed with the fear of making an error. They'd hold off treatment until he could give his personal okay. Do you think that's so hot for the patient? As for what it does to the students' psyches! Do you think it does society as a whole any good if they quit under the strain?"

"You sound bitter about him."

"Do I? I don't mean to. He didn't bother me. Felt

he was unbalanced, that's all. There's no doubt he was the best in his field if you needed surgery. And he was the man to learn from, too, if you had guts of steel. Patients who knew his reputation had absolute confidence in him. Of course they didn't get much in the way of bedside manner."

"Tell me what you remember from this evening."

"Well, he was dead. Noticed it right away. Jaw had dropped."

"You didn't first notice that he wasn't breathing?"

"No. He didn't respond when I went to say goodbye. That wasn't like him. He always wanted the last word."

"How did you happen to go over to him?"

"To say good-bye. I just told you that."

"But you could have called from where you were."

"Well, I may have, at first. But I walked up to him because it was more polite. After all, he was my host."

"How did you happen to circle around to his right?"

"Because the table was on his left and he was leaning toward his right. What are you implying? I didn't circle around and stab him. The blood was already dry."

"We know that. I was trying to find out whether you noticed anything else. Did anything attract your attention so that you went around to the right side?"

"Only that I'd already said something or other to him, and he hadn't responded."

DeGraaf spoke. "You said, 'Adam, we're going to leave. Thanks for the evening.'"

"Oh. So I did. Then I went over to him, around the back of the chair, and looked closer. There was the handle in his head, you know. Not exactly what I'd expected to see. Gave me a start. I called Melanie. I wouldn't usually do that to a girl, but after all, she's a pathologist. She might be upset about her father, but blood wouldn't worry her."

"I'm sure you did the right thing with Melanie," said DeGraaf.

"Well. And then, we just waited."

I said, "What about the earlier part of the evening? Did you notice anything? Anybody sneak up on Dr. Cotton? Any moans? Anybody act peculiar?"

"People were walking around all the time. And a lot of the time alone, because the two tables were not necessarily doing the same thing at the same time. One table would be bidding while the other would be playing the hand so that the one who was dummy was free to wander. See what I mean?"

"Yes. Did you see anybody come in the door?"

"I don't think so. Can't say I noticed anybody. You mean the butler?" he asked eagerly.

"I don't mean anybody especially."

"No, I don't think he ever came back in."

"Let me get this straight. You had your back to the windows, and therefore practically faced the door. And you did not see anybody come in?"

"Exactly."

Alec Spruance squirmed.

"Are you staying here, Mr. Spruance?" I asked mendaciously. I was hoping that addressing the wriggling kid as "Mr." would bring out some information.

"I'm signed out to my uncle," he said, fixing his eyes on my left shoe.

"What on earth does that mean?"

"When you sign out of school to a relative's, you can call and let them know if you're going to stay another night. They know where to call and check up on you, see?"

"So you're going to stay longer than you had planned?"

"Sure. It isn't as boring here right now as it usually is."

"I would think not. I can see you're not too broken up."

"I called him my uncle, but he wasn't. He was the brother of my aunt. Should I pretend to be broken up?"

"Didn't you like him?" DeGraaf asked, butting into my line of thought.

"Ha!"

"Could you be more verbal about it?" he asked.

"He was a real bastard. How's that for verbal?"

"Fabulous. He was paying your way through school, wasn't he?"

"Sure he was. And he could spare it without hurting. Made him feel good, too."

The fact that this was probably true didn't make the boy sound more appetizing to me. DeGraaf went on:

"Possibly he never let you forget it?"

"I'll say! I guess you knew him. Everything was fine as long as you did it his way."

"Yes, I've heard that."

"I did poorly in geometry last semester. So he said I had to take accounting this term. Accounting! I can't stand it. He said I would have to build my accuracy and my ability to concentrate. I don't like accounting and I'm failing it. I never failed a course in my whole life. It'll completely ruin my record!"

"Would he have managed your college career also?"

"I suppose—" A crafty look came over the kid's face. "No. I wouldn't have let him. I'm getting too old for that. It's ridiculous to think he'd have managed my life forever."

I said, "Could we get back to what happened here this evening? Where were you sitting?"

"At *his* table," he said, shrugging a shoulder at DeGraaf.

"Okay. What did you see?"

"The damn cards. It's stupid to play cards when half the world is starving."

"Let's talk about that some other time. What could you see in the room?"

"Well, I was sideways to the room. I could see Uncle Adam—I've been *taught* to call him Uncle Adam by Aunt Helen—I could see him if I turned all the way around to my right. But only the back of his chair, I suppose. Frankly, I didn't want to see him. I didn't see anybody creeping around with a knife."

"Who got up?"

"Who didn't? I think *he* stayed in his chair." Another shrug at DeGraaf. "I got up. So did Melanie. The old lady at our table did too. Maybe a couple of times."

"Mrs. Coyne?"

"Yes."

"I guess I saw Aunt Helen standing by the fire for a while. And the other old guy got up." Alec was determined not to dignify these people by admitting that he remembered their names. "And Peter. And the Arab character. They all got up, I guess."

"What did they do?"

"I didn't notice."

"Not at all?"

"No. Why should I? They weren't important or anything."

I sighed. "They are now."

"I'll bet they all say they went to get a drink."

"Didn't they?"

"Far as I know. I didn't notice, I told you."

"All right. What did you do when you got up?"

"Stretched my legs."

"Get a drink?"

"I guess so."

"Go to the fire?"

"I don't remember. I don't think so."

"Well, that's just great, kid. Saw nothing, heard nothing."

"I didn't go to Uncle Adam's end of the room. Maybe the guy who came in saw something."

DeGraaf and I did not glance at each other. "What person came in?"

"I don't know."

"Are you telling me you saw somebody, other than the eight card players and your uncle, come into that room?"

"Yes. I thought I noticed somebody."

"What did he look like?"

"I wasn't paying attention."

"Man or woman?"

"I don't know. This is silly. I shouldn't have mentioned it. I thought I saw somebody come in while we were playing bridge. But it could have been Johns or Mrs. Johns or anybody. How was I supposed to know I'd be asked questions about it later?"

DeGraaf said, "That's a perfectly legitimate point, Mr. Spruance. "Of course, you realize we have to hope some people noticed more than they had strict reason to."

"Sure."

"You can leave now if you want. Would you ask the officer to send somebody else in?" DeGraaf now and then forgets that he is here on my permission, and he is not in charge. The kid left. I let him go. What could you make of him anyway?

"I thought," said DeGraaf, "that as soon as somebody claimed to have seen a mysterious stranger, you were going to pounce."

"This one didn't seem to fill the bill."

"He didn't fill any bill. Don't you think any normal seventeen year old boy, having seen all the detective shows on television, would be bursting with theories about how the deed was done? Wouldn't he be dying to show us how observant he was and how many clues he'd noticed? He should have had the thing solved the moment he walked in here. Why didn't he?"

"He sure wasn't thrown off stride because of love for Adam Cotton."

"No. He was trying to project an image, and it wasn't a very convincing one."

A few minutes had gone by and still nobody came in to be plucked. I was about to tell Turgid, who was still sitting faithfully with his note pad in hand, to go yell at somebody, when the second uniformed man came to the door.

"Sir, I wish you'd come to the dining room. We don't know quite what to do about this."

I followed him and DeGraaf followed me. Turgid stayed, not having been given counter-orders. We could hear sobbing before we even got to the dining room. Inside, Mrs. Spruance was doubled up in a chair, shaking and crying, and Melanie was standing next to her rubbing her hand. Peter Erikson was leaning over her on the other side, saying, "Aunt Helen, nothing is going to happen to you. How would it be if I gave you a sleeping pill?"

"My life is over," the woman gulped.

Melanie said, "Aunt Helen, I'll take care of you. Please stop crying. Here's the inspector." She turned and put her hand on my elbow. "I really don't think she can talk to you, Inspector. She's too upset."

"What caused this?"

"Well, it's been brewing for the last half hour. At first she was just trembling a little, and then she started to cry."

"What's she afraid of?"

"I can't say, exactly," Melanie answered cautiously.

"Okay. I'm not going to browbeat anybody, if she's really ill. But if she knows something and she's just trying to hold back—"

Erikson came forward. "We don't think so. She certainly hasn't said anything you'd be interested in. Your officer has been here all the time, too."

I turned to the man and he nodded.

"I'd like to give her something to make her sleep," Erikson said.

Melanie added, "And I'll get her to bed. You can talk to Peter while I'm tucking her in and then I'll be down."

"We need her fingerprints."

"Did that," said the other officer. "Did everybody. Shall I take 'em downtown?"

"Yeah. Do that and get to work on them. Tell me something, Dr. Erikson."

"Yes?"

"Was it just after he took her prints that she really went to pieces?"

"I don't think that's fair," Melanie said. "She's been this way since it happened."

Erikson appeared to have dispensed with the sleeping pill idea, probably because the woman was gulping and sobbing so severely. He just took a hypo out of his bag and pushed up her sleeve. She was wearing a soft flowing sort of fabric and it took only a couple of seconds to inject the sedative.

"Give her until noon tomorrow, if you will," he said. "She won't really be functioning until then."

Melanie half-walked, half-carried the older woman to the door.

"Sergeant, help them up the stairs," I said.

Aunt Helen moaned, but the two got her moving. We heard the gasping and hiccupping fade as they moved down the hall. I turned around and suddenly noticed Dr. Passim hunched in a corner on a straight chair.

"How'd you get here?"

"I walked from the room—the study—where I talk with you. Is this wrong?"

"He wanted to ask me some questions, Inspector," said Erikson. "Dr. Passim was worried. There are parts of the world where the police might frame an outsider like he is. And he has also heard stories about Chicago—"

"Certainly. Who has not?" asked Passim innocently.

"I have been reassuring him that nothing is going to be pinned on him. And then when Aunt Helen became so upset he just waited."

"Okay, okay. What can I do now? Get along home, Passim. Nothing is going to happen to you if you haven't brought anything on yourself."

"Thank you, sir."

I turned to Erikson, who suddenly flashed a grin at me. It wasn't that I had overlooked him before, but I'd been busy. I could feel my sudden prejudice. This kind of thing I didn't need, and I fought it. It was just that the man was too handsome. His hair was gold, rich and boyish. It waved just enough to look great and not enough to look deliberately styled. He had perfect white teeth and a square jaw, tanned skin, dark blue eyes.

My dislike, or resentment, was not reasonable, and I tried to put it behind me.

He was talking:

"I guess I should tell you while Melanie is away —she would never say this herself if she could help it. But she wouldn't mind me making it clear. Aunt Helen is not upset about what you may think. She couldn't possibly have killed Cotton."

"How do you know?"

"She's too timid. The reason for her emotional outburst is that she's afraid with him gone she might not have a home here any longer. The irony is that it was Cotton who gave her that fear and Melanie who has always stood up for her. He always let her know that he kept her here out of charity; that she wasn't really needed. And that gave her an irrational fear of the future. Melanie wouldn't like to say that about her father, but he *was* that kind of a man."

"So Mrs. Spruance is safer now that he's dead?"

"Yes, but that's no motive for murder on her part. She doesn't even realize it yet. Because she had an argument with Cotton yesterday and he made some remark about her uselessness, she's jumped to the conclusion that Melanie might consider it her father's last wish that Aunt Helen leave. It's utter foolishness. The shock has made her irrational. Melanie knows perfectly well that her father said things like that all the time without meaning to carry them out. And besides that, she's really fond of her aunt. Never having had a mother, you know."

"Can you tell me the family background?" De-Graaf asked.

"Do you mean way back or what?"

"When did her mother die and what's the situation been since then?"

"Her mother died in an automobile accident twenty-five years ago, when Melanie was five. Dr. Cotton was either very saddened or very annoyed about it. I've never quite decided which."

"In what sense?"

"Maybe I shouldn't have said that. I suppose it's always been my impression that he was a very self-ish man," he said slowly. "That he was upset by his wife's death because it wasn't in accordance with his plans, not because of love for her. He wanted a son very much."

"And he had a daughter."

"Exactly. Melanie's always loved him. She's tried to be a son to him in some ways. Going into his profession, talking shop with him, and so on. But it wasn't what *he* had in mind. I think he was angry at his wife for getting herself killed before she had a boy or two."

"And Aunt Helen Spruance—when did she come into the picture?"

"Not long after. Her husband had died of pneumonia. She was Adam Cotton's only sister. Only sibling, for that matter. And she became sort of an unpaid housekeeper."

"So she's been here years and years?"

"Over twenty I'd say."

I was outraged. "And he was *still* threatening to throw her out?" I said.

"You have to realize Dr. Cotton liked to keep everybody up to snuff. He criticized a lot. Everybody from Melanie on down."

"Even you?"

"Sure, even me." Erikson grinned, with lots of teeth. "I didn't mind. I thought he was an interesting old devil. He knew about things. He wrote. The things he could tell you about the history of medicine—and of course, I wasn't dependent on him, as Aunt Helen was."

"What exactly did he say to her?"

As Erikson hesitated, DeGraaf said, "I think I know the kind of thing. Tonight he said something about too few large logs being laid out for the fire. Then he told her she had little enough to do around the house and ought to be able to get it right."

"Exactly," Erikson said sadly, with his firm chin nicely squared. "It wasn't a kind thing to say. And he wasn't a kind sort of person. But he wouldn't have turned her out of the house either."

We had walked slowly back towards the study with Erikson, and Turgid took up his pen and began taking notes as we walked in, though we were in the mid-stream of the conversation. We were just sorting ourselves out to sit when Erikson caught sight of the scalpel on a sheet of paper on the desk.

"Was that it?" he asked.

I said it was, and watched him.

"I was afraid so when I saw it in his head, but I wasn't sure. And I wanted to get Melanie away from there rather than stand around and make sure."

"Why? Are you familiar with this scalpel?"

"It's either the one Adam used as a letter opener or one exactly like it."

That tore it. If the thing had been in the house or worse yet on the coffee table near Cotton's hand all evening, then we couldn't trace the knife to any one of the suspects. What was more, it opened the possibility that the crime, rather than planned, had been a crime of impulse, based on the sudden realization by the killer that the circumstances made it possible. And the less preparation, generally the fewer traces left behind. I asked Erikson, "You say it's either Adam Cotton's or like his. Aren't they all alike?"

"I thought you knew. There are dozens, maybe hundreds of scalpels and scalpel-like knives used in surgery. There are different blade types for different uses, and several handle types too, depending on the manufacturer. And the preference of the surgeon, of course. Surgeons can be prima donnas, you know, and they get very definite about the feel of the handle and which ones they like. This is a Ferris-Smith. It was developed by a plastic surgeon. I never knew why Adam had that type, particularly since he can't use it much in vascular work. Maybe just because the blade is longer than most, so it made a good letter-opener."

"Hell. Well, let's go on. Who was in a position to kill him? What went on in there tonight?"

Erikson glanced at DeGraaf, but refrained from saying that I could get the story from him. "I've assumed it was an outsider."

"Did you see any strangers come in?"

"No. Not even the butler. But I was sitting far back in the corner. The bookcase was between Cotton and me. I had a long diagonal view of the door across the room, but I wasn't looking at it. There was plenty of opportunity for a person to come in unseen—or unnoticed, at least. People got up and walked around, but not constantly. There were long periods when no one was up. And people study their cards when they're playing bridge; their attention is not on the other side of the room. Besides, if someone came into the room, each player would think it was either somebody from the other table or the butler."

"Unless he happened to look."

"Of course. Even then I suppose it would look like Cotton just had a visitor. The person, wouldn't be challenged or stopped."

"It would have been risky."

"Whoever did this took some risks."

"Touché. What if we find that nobody saw any such stranger?"

"Then nobody looked up."

"Well, it's consistent, as an explanation. Is there anything relevant you can tell us about anyone's movements in there this evening?"

"Not a thing."

"Okay. Thank you, Dr. Erikson. Would you see whether Melanie Cotton is back from upstairs, and ask her to come in?"

Melanie looked about as tired and haggard as anybody with freckles can. Her hands were jammed into the pockets of her blue denim suit and she had her lower lip caught between her teeth. Her short chestnut hair was rumpled. I found myself softening my voice when I talked: "Sorry to have to ask you questions this evening, Miss Cotton—Dr. Cotton."

"No, please don't be. It's just as well to get it over with."

"Of course, while events are fresh in everybody's minds, the details are much more accurate."

"Of course. Please go ahead."

"Let's cover the ground with the basics. You were sitting where?"

"Well, with my back to the east wall. That was to Dr. DeGraaf's right. I think the important thing is that I could see my father's chair and everything at that end of the room."

"Everything meaning—"

"Meaning the fire, the table with the drinks, the coffee table near Dad, the door. The chair Dad was sitting in, but not him, because of the way it was turned, with its back toward us. I noticed his hand reach out a couple of times."

"How late in the evening was that?"

"How late? Oh, I see. You want to decide what time he was killed?"

"Yes."

"Well, the problem is, I was noticing more during the first half of the game. There got to be a sort of problem at our table later on, and I was worrying about it. Not paying much attention to anything else. I wish I had!"

"What sort of problem at your table?"

"Oh, hasn't he told you?" she looked at DeGraaf. "It was Alec. He was being difficult."

"Difficult in what way?"

"Alec always wants to win at everything, but he doesn't take the trouble to learn how to do it right. So of course he fails. He expects a brilliant flash or something to come and help him out at the last minute. But there aren't any such things." She spoke with the unconscious scorn of one who by nature takes pains and gets things right. She was probably a very good pathologist. "When Alec kept

going down, in spite of the fact that it was happening because he overbid his hand, he got
angry."

"What did you do about it?"

"Just tried to keep the conversation cheerful, I
guess."

DeGraaf cut in. "How did you feel about being
on a team that lost in that way?"

"What a strange question! I felt—I didn't object
to it, as long as I didn't make any mistakes myself."

"Did you regret having Alec as a partner?"

"I thought it was my duty to take him as a partner, rather than inflict him on a guest. I grabbed
him right at the beginning. I've seen him play lots
of times before, you know."

"We're wandering from the point," I said. "Let's
get back to the question of when you last saw your
father reach for something."

"Very early, I think. During the first or second
hand. I went over to him early in the evening too,
when I was dummy. I asked him whether he wanted
anything more to drink. He was all right then."

"So you know he was alive up to the third or
fourth hand?"

"That's right."

"What about the other people? What did they do
during bridge?"

"Mr. Craddock, if I had seen somebody go over
there and stab my father, don't you think I would
have done something about it?" All at once there
was an edge of hysteria in her voice.

"Steady, Melanie," DeGraaf said. "After all,
somebody did do it somehow. Rob only wants to
know whether you saw anybody near your father for
a long time or doing anything that was unex-
plainable at the time."

"I know. I'm sorry. I realize all that. But she—that is, anybody—all the people here tonight are good people. They wouldn't do such a thing. It must have been an outsider."

"How could an outsider get in?"

"The door wasn't locked. It was only shut."

I glanced at DeGraaf, but he was watching the girl. We didn't say anything about the butler. "Dr. Cotton, did you see anybody come in?"

"No, but I might not have. Maybe nobody did. That doesn't prove there wasn't such a person."

"Right. Right."

DeGraaf took over. "What did you mean when you said 'she' just now?"

"When?"

"You started to say who wouldn't have done it. You said 'she' and then you changed it to everybody.

"I don't know what you mean," said Melanie. Then she held her breath and turned pink. She wasn't a good liar.

"Look, Melanie" said DeGraaf, "more than one person has mentioned seeing your Aunt Helen standing for quite some time near the fire. Is that what you mean? She's not going to be arrested for looking at a fire, after all."

Melanie let out the breath. "All right. Yes, it is. I didn't think about it until later. I thought it would give you the wrong impression. After all, it's quite natural for a person to stand and look at a fire, isn't it? I did it myself."

"How long was she there?"

"I wasn't really keeping track. What surprised me, thinking of it later, was that I looked up a couple of times and she was still there. You'd think she'd want to know how her team was doing."

"Did you see her go over to your father?"

"Never!" She seemed to think we doubted her, for she added, "I really didn't! She never even moved. She stood so awfully still. That was what made me remember it."

"All right," I said. "What about the rest of the guests?"

"You mean where everybody went? It's the same problem. I was so intent on avoiding a scene. That is, we'd had a scene, but it could have been worse. If he had absolutely refused to go on playing, for instance. That would have left three of us unable to play and it would have spoiled the duplicate aspect for both tables, too."

"So you didn't notice what *anybody* did?"

"No, I don't mean that. But I only noticed a few things. I'm pretty sure, for instance, that Dr. De-Graaf never got up at all. I know Alec got up at least once, when I was playing the hand, because I remember being relieved that he was gone. I was paying attention to him."

"And on top of that, he was rude to you when he sat back down," DeGraaf said.

"Yes, but you have to overlook that. He can't stand to see anybody else win if he's losing."

"Life to him must be filled with difficult sights."

For some reason that drew the first smile from her. "He is awful, isn't he? But he's young."

I said, "What about the others?"

"Um—Mrs. Coyne got up once or twice, I think. And Dr. Coyne at least once. I saw somebody go to the fire, but I don't remember who. And I think somebody spoke to my father. I guess that's not much help."

"I don't know," I sighed. "I suppose it's the best we could hope for. If anybody had seen the stabbing, he'd have spoken up at the time. And if they had seen something odd, they'd still have mentioned it to the first policeman who came through the door. Or to you, Gerritt, for that matter."

He said, "Unless they had good reason not to."

"Like what?"

"Like husbands and wives don't tell on each other. Or relatives sometimes, or even engaged couples. Don't be upset, Melanie, please. I'm not suggesting anything specific. I haven't the foggiest idea how this death took place. I'm just saying that people don't always blurt out all they know. And you should know that better than any of us, Rob."

I humphed at him.

"I don't care about that," Melanie said. "I'm not disturbed if you do suspect us. Any of us. But I want you to find out who did it, and punish him. I should be too civilized to say that, but I'm not!"

To my amazement she burst into tears, jumped and ran out of the room.

After a silence, I said, "Well, that's our last witness."

"Yup. There we are."

"Yup. Nowhere."

"Of course, we haven't spoken to Aunt Helen Spruance."

I frowned at him. "What with the statement from the butler that nobody went into that room all evening—all right, all right, I know I'm going to talk with the gardener. But Johns wouldn't have said it if Pryczyk wouldn't confirm it. And if they're honest witnesses, it is absolutely conclusive that one of the eight people playing bridge is the killer."

"Okay."

"So we just wait for the fingerprint report and find out who it was."

"Just like that. Bingo."

There was a knock at the door. I shouted, "Come in," and the uniformed officer entered.

"Fingerprints called on the car radio for you, sir."

"Ask and you shall receive. We're almost home, Gerritt. All right, Olert, which one did he say did it?"

"Which of what, sir?"

"Never mind. Just repeat the message."

"He says that he has made a preliminary comparison of the prints of the parties in the room at the time of the deceased—decession—the death—with the prints on the knife, sir. And he added that he had the butler's, the cook's, and the gardener's prints also."

"I know that. What was the result?"

"None of them match, sir."

"What?"

"None of them match, sir."

"You said that. With the knife prints?"

"That's right, sir. The prints on the knife weren't made by any of those people."

# CHAPTER FOUR

For several seconds I was numb. Then I started thinking and as I did I could feel my face get hot. I didn't want to look at DeGraaf. I didn't want to say anything. Then I heard him laugh.

"Rob, you should see the changes your face just went through," he said. "The one I liked best was when Realization of the Possibilities swept over it."

I still didn't look at him.

He said, "Turgid, I think you'd better get your print kit out of the car. And take my prints."

Turgid looked at me for instructions. I nodded. The officer turned on his heel and went out. Now I was feeling like a fool. DeGraaf is not a killer. And he wouldn't ask to have his prints taken if the ones on the knife were his.

The officer was back, thank heaven, in a minute and a half. I couldn't have sat there not quite facing DeGraaf for very long. I stared blankly at the head of a leopard while DeGraaf, who naturally knew how, rolled his fingers methodically on the ink pad and the paper, one of each finger in each of the labelled spaces.

"Shall I rush 'em directly in to Prints, sir?" Turgid asked cheerfully.

"Oh, Jeez, no. Drop 'em off when you check out this evening. It's only a formality anyway."

Turgid went out to store the stuff in the car. There was an awkward chuckle. Then DeGraaf started laughing again. After a moment I smiled too.

"Well, the idea gave me a shock for a minute," I said, fairly unnecessarily.

"I could tell."

"Actually, I don't suppose we even have to match them."

"It'll clear the air."

"Oh, hell, I never thought you killed him, Gerritt. I can't imagine why you'd even want to. And you're the one person who never got up all evening. Everybody agrees to that."

"Yes—"

"It was just that, as soon as I thought I'd proven that somebody in the room killed him, suddenly it turns out that nobody could have."

"Exactly. I was about to say, it wouldn't be much more of a miracle for me to have done it sitting in my chair than for an unknown and unseen person to walk past two able bodied men."

"You're not saying—"

"No, I didn't kill him. I hardly even knew him."

"You said able bodied men. Maybe I'd better give Johns and Pryczyk an eye test."

"Oh, come on, Rob. That hall isn't more than five feet wide. Neither one of them would be able to do his job if he were that blind."

"I guess. I guess."

"Besides, the floor is hardwood. They'd hear anybody who walked on it, unless he took off his shoes. And that would be courting attention by the bridge players. I am willing to consider somebody who looked like a butler being overlooked, but not a barefoot butler."

"I know. So it must have been a ghost."

As soon as I said it, I wished I hadn't. I have absolutely no nerves at all—you can't and last in this business. But that house was just too dark. It's halls were too narrow, too echoing, and the heads of dead animals kept looking at me. To make it all worse, DeGraaf himself looked uneasy. Maybe a whiff of what had really happened, a distant smell of the brimstone, came to him right then.

But after a few seconds he said, brightly, "Well, let's look at this sensibly. Could anybody have been hiding under the refreshment table or in the bookcase?"

"No, and you know it. There's no tablecloth on the refreshment table. Anybody crouching under it would be seen right away. And the bookcases are deep but open. No doors, no cabinets."

"What about someone climbing in the window?"

"Gerritt, please! *You* were facing the only window that was open. And it was open two inches! *Nobody* concentrates so hard they don't see a man climbing in a window. It's not an accepted way to crash a party."

"All right, you think of something. You're just complaining and worrying about ghosts."

"So?"

"And another thing. I have a feeling we'd better eliminate everything possible, however ridiculously remote, right now. Because the time is going to come when we're going to want to narrow this down to the least unlikely explanation. And when that time comes, you won't want any loose ends flapping around."

"I know."

"And we'll be running around in circles, saying it had to be an insider, but it couldn't be an insider, so it had to be an outsider, but it couldn't have been an outsider, so it had to be an insider—"

"All right. All right. We'd better take a hard look at the room."

It is natural to the human mind to expect the rooms where murders have taken place to be tainted. Therefore, they are usually disappointing. People have a psychological need to see something larger than life, to feel a current in the air where passions strong enough to cause murder have passed. But in fact these rooms are like any room, painted or panelled or wallpapered, dusty or clean, elegant or shabby, large or small, just like anyplace else.

So when I entered the library and felt my scalp prickle, I shivered. The fingers of a dead hand passed down my back. I looked behind me and saw DeGraaf, a few steps back, look behind himself too. We pretended we were checking the view from the bench in the hall.

I was determined to take a thorough survey of the place. Unfortunately, the room had not altered to the extent of providing me with brand-new inspiration.

The fireplace was in the center of the South wall. Directly in front of it was the coffee table. Slightly past that, to the west but facing the fire, was Adam Cotton's chair. There, on the coffee table, was

Cotton's manuscript, and the glass he had been drinking from, a little brandy still inside. The glass had been printed—there was still dust on it—but I realized I had not had the contents analyzed. I went to the door and bellowed.

The door I leaned out of was the only door in the room. It was in the east wall, but in the corner, near the fire. In other words, anybody entering would have to pass in front of the fire to get to Cotton's chair. This seemed important to me, because it would alter the light as seen by the card players and attract their attention.

North of the door, the refreshment table was set up against the east wall. It was an oak table with turned spindle legs. The top was covered with glasses and bottles, but the floor under it was bare and visible.

In the north wall were the two tall windows, one open a couple of inches. Under each window was a card table and four folding chairs. The remaining wall, the west, was all floor-to-ceiling bookcases, and jutting out from the wall halfway along was the bookcase that blocked the view of Cotton from the second card table—a floor-to-ceiling bookcase matching the others. All were crammed with books. There was a stool in the corner for getting books from top shelves. It was unmistakably a library.

I'd get Turgid to make a formal floor plan of the place tomorrow for our files. But for now a few things were obvious. A man could be killed at one end of the room, and if the killing were silent, people at the other end would not notice. The room was long enough, maybe thirty feet, to make that feasible. DeGraaf saw me studying the length and made another point. "The way this place is divided, it's psychologically two rooms. The bookcase and the refreshment table contribute to the effect, but so does the lighting. At that end there's the fire and Cotton's reading lamp. At this end there are two bright lights, one hung over each card table. Because of the extra lighting here, Cotton's end was comparatively dim. The arrangement of furniture and the lighting would both make a person's attention stay inside his closer area."

"That doesn't mean no one would see somebody come in."

"I didn't say it would. As a matter of fact, I'm pretty certain several of them would have noticed. It would have been an interruption, a definite change. All I meant was that if somebody who was dummy did the killing, nobody need notice."

"I was thinking so myself."

"And because nobody, or maybe only Alec, noticed an intruder, I don't think there was one."

"And therefore we have an impossible murder."

"So far."

I did not find this especially satisfying, even though DeGraaf seemed pleased with it.

Well, all right, who would have seen what? I sat for a moment in DeGraaf's bridge chair. His view was straight out the slightly opened window. No man could have crawled in that window unnoticed. I went to Melanie's chair. With her back to the east wall, she could see her father's chair, just as she had told us. She was right next to the table of drinks, and beyond it she could see the door.

Mrs. Coyne's seat, with her back to the window, faced the fire, but at a distance, of course. She could see the back of Cotton's chair, the fire, the coffee table, the refreshment table—everything important except a small triangle of space behind the jutting bookcase.

Sliding into Alec Spruance's chair, I made a minor discovery. He faced Melanie and the east wall. Looking just slightly to his right, he'd be staring at the refreshment table. But as far as the other end of the room was concerned—Cotton, the door and the fire—he would have to look right to see the door and so far right as to have to turn partly around if he wanted to see Cotton. So why was his memory of whether people got drinks so sketchy? And why was he the one to see a stranger? His memory of one side of the room was too good, of the other side too poor.

I thought I'd reserve my suspicions of Alec for a while. I knew DeGraaf had dismissed him as a possible killer, and it wouldn't hurt our relationship if I could steal a march on DeGraaf for once.

This pleasant hope was dampened when I remembered that nobody in here could have done it. For the sake of completeness, I sat in the four chairs at the other table. Their positions coincided in every way with what people had told us. In fact, all had described what they saw from the appropriate angles. Of all the accounts, only Alec's seemed improbable in view of where he sat.

Which left it all up in the air.

"You know," said DeGraaf, who had been wandering around aimlessly, "Nobody, when we were sitting down, could see into that corner formed by the bookcase that juts out from the other bookcases against the wall. It's a little triangle right behind Cotton's chair."

I hurried over to look. "I can't believe you wouldn't have seen if somebody was standing there. You all stood around the fire having drinks, didn't you?"

"Yes, I know. It's probably nothing."

"Of course, Cotton's reading lamp isn't bright. There's a shadow in that corner. No, it's impossible. Anybody standing pressed into the corner would be pretty suspicious."

"You're absolutely right. It's another case of eliminating everything. Beside the fact that we would have seen him earlier in the evening, where would he have gone after the murder? Anybody coming in the window or hiding under a table would have the same problem of getting away. If Johns and Pryczyk didn't see anybody enter or leave, he must still be here. And he isn't."

"He got out after the murder was discovered. When you called Johns and told him about the murder. Everybody was too upset to notice."

"Oh, Rob, don't be silly. By that time we were all at this end of the room, milling around. And we were alerted, you know. And if that weren't enough, most of the people here were not extremely upset or distracted. Cotton was not a well-liked man."

"Still, there'd be confusion."

"Not enough. There's only one door. I was standing by the body. Coyne stood near the door. Rob, if you're going to believe anything that anybody says, you're going to have to believe what everyone will tell you—and already has told you by implication. From the time the body was found, no stranger left this room."

"So it's all a washout."

DeGraaf went purposefully over to Cotton's chair by the fire and sat down.

I said, "So?"

"First, I don't see anyone in the room from here,

unless it's a person standing within two feet of the fire, or possibly if he sat on the coffee table, which is hardly likely."

"A little conspicuous, I would think."

"No doubt. Or I would see a person who came around the right arm of the chair, which would not be so conspicuous. Anyone who wanted to talk quietly with Cotton during the bridge game would do that, rather than hang over the coffee table. It is exactly what the murderer must have done."

"Didn't I hear you making it sound unlikely to circle around on Cotton's left when you were talking with Coyne an hour ago?"

"You did, but the situation wasn't the same. If several people are playing cards seriously, you don't start a loud conversation in the room. You might walk around the far side of a man's chair if you could get closer to him that way, to talk quietly, so as not to disturb anyone else. But when we were all getting ready to leave, it was different. We could raise our voices. After all, a restrained degree of boisterousness is taken to mean that everybody had a good time. Secondly, Coyne was already speaking loudly. He talks in a near shout. So it would be reasonable to expect him to shout at Cotton then, and in fact he did."

"All right. Then he didn't get any answer, so he went around and looked."

"Sure. But Cotton was cantankerous and might have preferred to stay absorbed in his work. Or he might have fallen asleep. In either case, his daughter and sister were both available to be thanked. There was no special *need* to wake him up, or break into his grouch, or whatever."

"Maybe. It's also reasonable to think something

is wrong if a person doesn't answer after a while."

"Sure, if it were half a minute or so."

"And it wasn't?"

"No."

"Aha!"

"Rob, don't jump to conclusions. I only pushed Coyne on it because it seemed a little unnecessary. His answer was adequate. He's officious, not that he'd put it that way. He would go to see Cotton, while another person would put the silence down as rudeness, let it pass, and discreetly extend his thanks to the daughter instead."

"Everything we touch goes nowhere. Shall we call it a night?"

"I wish we would."

This wasn't like Gerritt. I looked more closely at him. Now, DeGraaf is a man who will go anywhere anytime if he thinks there's an item of interest at the end of the trip. And he does not tire. But that night he looked gray. He saw me looking at him, but all he said was, "Let's get out of here."

"Are you sick?"

"No. I just don't like this. Probably things'll look brighter in the morning."

In the hall, however, we ran into Melanie Cotton and Peter Erikson, standing together, looking fragile. They were holding hands. For a moment I wondered whether Erikson was going to criticize us for making Melanie cry, but he didn't. Both were too concerned with genuine problems for that.

I said immediately, "I'm going to station a man in that room. I'm sorry it's necessary, but there are a number of peculiar problems here. I don't want anybody going in there. Not even to clean."

"I understand," Melanie said. She caught her

breath to go on, but Erikson beat her to it.

"I don't suppose you know yet who killed him—no, that's silly. I'm sure you'll tell us when you do. I'm being incoherent, but I wanted to say both of us will do anything to help."

"Yes, really," Melanie said. "You *have* to find out who did it."

"It's Melanie's father, and not only that, but the other people too," Erikson said. "We want to find out for his sake. And to protect the other people who were in that room. They'll all be suspected until this is cleared up. And that's not fair."

"Not fair at all," Melanie added, unnecessarily. I thought this adding of unnecessary words did more than anything else to show her distress. I imagine she was usually a most efficient speaker, a compact, efficient girl altogether. Now she was meandering.

Erikson must have known it too, which is hardly amazing since he knew her better than I did. I'd never seen her under normal circumstances. "Melanie is going right to bed with a sleeping pill," he said. "Inspector, I know you've got a car outside, but Dr. DeGraaf—maybe I could give you a lift?"

"No, thanks. I have my car, too," said DeGraaf. "And I couldn't stand to be pumped on this thing right now. My brain is too confused."

"I didn't mean—"

"No, don't apologize. It's completely natural to want to talk about it. I'll catch you tomorrow. Good night."

# CHAPTER FIVE

I called him early the next morning. Although I wasn't worried about him, the first thing I asked was how he felt.

"I don't know what it was," he said. "It was like that expression, 'There's someone walking over my grave.' It went away when I left the house."

"It's a good thing you don't have to do this every day, like me."

"Come on. You enjoy it. Nobody forced you to take your job. Didn't you have other talents?"

"As a teenager I was a very good spotter."

"What do you mean?"

"I worked at our local laundry in Elk Grove. I removed spots."

"Oh. *Plus ça change, plus c'est la même chose.*"

"Don't go fancy on me. I know that one. I called to ask you something and I'm in a hurry. Do you want to visit Mrs. Spruance with me?"

"Ah. She's over her vapors?"

"How do I know? It's ten after seven in the morning. I'll call later. But if she isn't she'd better be."

"What time do you want to go?"

"I figure after lunch; they can't possibly claim that she's still dopey then. Around one."

"Great. I have a class at ten, so that works."

What he did not add was that he had a few things to do on his own. He admitted it to me later.

Skipping breakfast, he hurried over to the hospital to look at the surgical schedules. The gods were playing it his way. Dr. Coyne had an artery graft scheduled for seven. It was now seven-forty. The operation would take about an hour. And since Coyne always had coffee in the cafeteria after surgery—DeGraaf had seen him there for years—things were well-ordered from DeGraaf's point of view.

He ran his eye down the pages to be certain Coyne didn't have a second procedure scheduled. But he didn't. That was all right. DeGraaf headed for the cafeteria with a definite schedule in mind. Breakfast at seven forty-five. Coffee with Coyne at eight or shortly after, though Coyne didn't know it yet. Plenty of time. Class at ten. Lunch with Erikson, if he could be waylaid. And then Aunt Helen Spruance. He particularly wanted to catch Coyne and Erikson, the two doctors, alone. He thought they would talk with him more freely in the absence of policemen.

Maybe so.

Not knowing how long he would have to wait, he stocked up on scrambled eggs, two Danishes, grilled ham, bagels, coffee, and a small orange juice. He balanced his tray and swivelled-hipped his way through tables filled with people who had just gotten off the eleven-to-seven shift: nurses, orderlies, aides, interns, doctors, the whole ant-heap in cross-section. The cup clattered on his tray and the coffee slopped over into the saucer as he snaked his way between discarded chairs and stepped over purses, books, and coats. But he was bound for a certain section of the room facing the elevators that came down from the O.R.s, and no ordinary, easy-to-reach table would do.

And he found one. It was a table for four, as they all were. He spread his breakfast in front of three of the chairs in an attempt to discourage unwanted visitors.

Of course it didn't work. He was just placing his orange juice and plate of ham in front of the third chair, when someone shouted "Hi!" in his ear.

"Hey, Gringo!" said DeGraaf.

"What're you doin'? Trying to keep people away?" said Gringo, eyeing the food.

"Yup."

"I'll tell you what I'm going to do for you. I'll sit in your fourth seat. That ought to help."

"Think I need help? Why?"

"You're such an innocent, Gerritt. The whole damn place is buzzing about what happened to Cotton. And you were *there* and now you're *here*. Look behind you."

DeGraaf turned around. Three nurses left a huddle and came his way. One was a pale, beautiful red-head he often worked with in Emergency.

"Gerritt, is it true that Dr. Cotton was murdered?" she asked for the three of them.

"I'm afraid it is."

"How? How did it happen?" she breathed, getting right to the vital problem.

"We can't tell yet."

"But tell me, what did *you* see?"

"There was a scalpel driven into his brain. How it happened, how it really happened, we don't know."

"Listen, people," Gringo said, "we've got an emergency to discuss—"

"Oh, you always have an emergency. That's what you do for a living," laughed the nurse. But she took the hint and the three wandered away, glancing back. A couple of doctors also edged closer, but Gringo waved them away and they veered off.

"You can't really blame them," said Gringo.

"I don't. The unbearable ghouls."

"People shouldn't be so curious. So what really did happen?"

DeGraaf gave the man a pitying stare. "Not above it either, are we? What do you think: could a man be stabbed in the temple and not even scream?"

"Sure. Easy. You know that. Just so long as it was done fast. I wonder whether most people would realize how little force was needed, though."

"Exactly. The skull is thin at the temple, but how many people would know it? Even if a layman looked up the skull in *Gray's Anatomy*, he wouldn't know its thickness from the pictures. I can't think of any readily available text that has cross sections of the parietal."

"Neither can I. Although you hear on every other television program that the temple is a dangerous place to be hit. Why do you need to know that so badly?"

"Oh, there were five doctors and three laymen there. I'd like to eliminate some of them."

"Like Mrs. Coyne?"

"Yes."

"She was a nurse."

"Oh. That's bad."

"From your point of view. I wouldn't eliminate any laymen, anyhow."

"Gringo, I'll take your word. The point is, this killer had to know that eight—no, seven—people sitting fifteen feet away wouldn't hear a scream or a groan."

Gringo whistled. "So it's true what they're all saying."

"If that's what they're saying, it's true. News sure travels fast."

"A hospital is like a village."

"Unnh." DeGraaf lit into his scrambled eggs and bagels.

"You know, it wouldn't matter so much that the killer *knew* that a deep knife thrust would kill instantly."

"No?"

"Not so long as he *believed* it would. It'll work whether or not you have specialized knowledge."

As Melanie told us that afternoon, about this time she was hiding in the pantry. She was getting away from her Aunt Helen.

Helen Spruance, once she awakened from the drug, had made a remarkable recovery from her panic of the night before and was determined to spend every waking hour protecting her niece. This was the very last thing Melanie needed. She wanted either to be let alone or to see Peter. But Peter would not be able to visit until early afternoon, after he had "settled down" all his cases, and meanwhile Aunt Helen would not let her alone.

Aunt Helen prepared cups of tea and delivered them to Melanie, although Melanie had always preferred coffee to tea and might well be expected to go on doing so.

"My dear, I know you're a fully grown woman. But you have not had a mother's touch, though I'm sure I've tried to be a mother to you. I hope you'll let me advise you in this awful period of your life."

"Certainly, Aunt Helen." Anything to turn off the flow of conversation.

"I don't know how we are supposed to plan for the funeral, not knowing when the police will let us —um—"

"Not knowing when they'll release the body?" Melanie helped her, wincing as she said it. Her aunt did not notice winces.

"Yes, yes. Exactly. I keep forgetting that you know all about these things. Why a perfectly attractive girl should go into that sort of job, I'll never know."

Melanie was longing to be at that very job, to take her mind off things. "Aunt Helen," she said, "they will release the body almost immediately. There's no problem about the identification, and a post mortem doesn't take long. Any arrangements we want to make, we can make right now. We could plan to hold the funeral in two or three days. Maybe sooner would be better."

"We wouldn't want to look hasty."

"Why don't you call the funeral director and discuss it?"

So Aunt Helen went to the phone and Melanie went to the pantry to hide. She leaned her head against a shelf. Why should it look bad for her to go to work? Work made her feel better, anytime. There was nothing in working that would dishonor her father. As it was, she felt trapped.

And then she heard feet coming, little nervous feet.

"Melanie! What are you doing in here?"

"Just thinking, Aunt Helen."

"Oh, really, dear, I wouldn't. It isn't good for you. Come in and sit down."

"I don't *want* to sit down, Aunt Helen."

"You'll upset yourself. Did you have any breakfast before I got up?"

"I don't remember."

"That means you didn't! I'll tell Mary Ellen to make you up some nice custard."

"Aunt Helen, I'm not *ill*."

"Well, you will be if you don't eat. A little custard never hurt anybody."

DeGraaf looked down at a deserted plate that had once held scrambled eggs. The bagel plate was empty too. So was the plate of Danish. He pulled over what was left of the ham, then, looking up, saw Coyne come out of the elevator.

"Hey, Gringo. Will you slip discreetly away?"

"What are friends for?"

Gringo went to the door as Coyne picked up a tray with a doughnut and coffee.

DeGraaf kept his eye fixed on his quarry. He was determined not to let him slip away, just in case Coyne might want to avoid him. As the other man finished paying, DeGraaf stood up and waved. Coyne saw him, nodded, and threaded his way over without any sign of wanting to escape.

"I thought you might want to get away from people who just want the gory details, Liam," DeGraaf said.

"Have you run into that, too, this morning?"

"Incessantly."

"Umm. Am I tired!" He sagged into a chair. His pink nose and cheeks looked purplish this morning. "I don't know why there's this mystique about operating at the crack of dawn."

"Long case?"

"No, not really. An artery graft. Motorcycle accident. And just a kid. I'm seeing more and more of them, and I'm not even in the field they usually need. Mostly cranial injuries. That's the usual thing. Oh, hell, I'm sorry. You know all this better than I do."

"I see a lot of it, that's for sure." Coyne spoke in a loud bark. DeGraaf could see people looking frankly at them, hoping to pick up something interesting. "Liam, speaking of being tired this morning, why do you suppose Adam Cotton would hold a dinner on a Sunday night, knowing perfectly well that most of the guests had to be at work early the next morning?"

Coyne laughed, rather nastily. "You know Adam."

"Actually, I hardly knew him at all."

"Oh, come on. You knew his reputation then. Hospitals are hotbeds of gossip."

Keeping his voice down, DeGraaf said, "I heard he was hard to get along with. So are a lot of people."

"Adam was something else again. Cold as a halibut. If he held parties on Sundays—and, by the way, I think I remember somebody being invited to his house on a Sunday last fall—"

"Melanie said he gives one about every six months."

"Yes." Coyne shook his head. "Queerest bug you

ever saw. Well, if he always did it on Sundays, it was so that he could have the reputation of holding occasional parties and therefore of not being a recluse, yet at the same time the guests would have to leave early. He wouldn't have to tolerate their presence too long."

"Nice."

"Just like him to set up the duplicate bridge hands, too. Make the rest of us jump through his hoop and yet not play himself."

"I see what you mean. How is vascular surgery muddling along without its chief?"

"Amicably."

"For a one-word answer, that says a lot." He looked at Coyne and saw how shadowed his eyes were. For all his frankness, there was something he wasn't saying. About Cotton or about himself?

"This Dr. Passim," DeGraaf said. "Wasn't he being trained by Cotton?"

"He's a graduate physician, a student from abroad, not any special protégé of Cotton's. Part of the teaching hospital philosophy, you know. He assisted me this morning. That's what he'll do. Put in his time with other people in the field. No problem."

"How does he feel about it?"

"You don't leave a person time for a gulp of coffee. Ibid is very relieved."

"Why should that be?"

"Well, I'll tell you. Ibid makes mistakes. I don't mean he kills patients. He doesn't have the authority to do that yet." Coyne started laughing, then couldn't stop, and laughed and laughed until tears came to his eyes. Thinking it would help, he took a large swallow of coffee, burned his tongue, grimaced, and sat still, very red in the face. "Mmp. Passim has a language problem. It's improving. But Cotton would ask him to hold this or retract that, and Ibid would sometimes grab the wrong thing first. Then Cotton would quietly swear at him. You know what happens when you do that to a student. He freezes up and then does *two* wrong things in succession. Unpleasant for the nurses, too. It's not that everybody is sweet and peaceful all the time. We all get angry. But Cotton did it routinely and he wasn't even angry, just coldly abusive."

"As a colleague, how do you rate Cotton's abilities?"

Coyne took a breath, then said, more quietly than usual, "He was the best there is."

While DeGraaf was teaching his class, he was also fidgeting with impatience. He wanted to be getting on with the Cotton affair, but he had an obligation to his students as well. So of course he overdid his duty to them.

He told them about the bad old days—and they were very recent—when the treatment of emergency room patients was not a specialty at all. In most hospitals staff physicians had simply covered the emergency room in rotation.

"Most small hospitals still do, and even some larger places that ought to know better and have the space to do better. Of course, you are all rotated through the emergency service at some point. But it doesn't follow from the fact that every doctor should know emergency procedures that every doctor, whatever his field, is qualified to give emergency care. It's a genuine specialty, and one you might consider going into. The amount of specialized emergency equipment is huge. It takes time to master it all. And the use of emergency rooms is way up. This is partly because many people find their doctor is unavailable when they need him or because they have no regular doctor. And some people realize that the ordinary doctor's office may not have emergency equipment like defilbrillators. But besides that, there are new emergencies—allergic reactions to hundreds of the new drugs, and injuries from types of industrial equipment that were unknown ten years ago. And chemical burns, inhalation, and absorption through the skin. Trauma surgery is itself completely different from scheduled surgery. The field is not sterile. Wounds are ragged. There can be foreign substances embedded in the injury. It's a mess. The previous condition of the patient is unknown and he may be unable to tell you. Allergies unknown. Medications unknown. Depth of the wound unknown. You're working in an area where you have to guess, under pressure, and with a lot at stake."

He stopped and grinned at his own enthusiasm. "Well—that's what makes it so damned interesting."

By eleven-thirty he was back in the cafeteria, perched, waiting for Peter Erikson to put in an appearance. He felt like an old hand at lying in wait with excessive food in front of him, but it was much more difficult now. The cafeteria was more crowded at lunch than in the morning, and not even the idea that he was on a quest of which the gods would approve made DeGraaf feel he would be justified in tying up four chairs when the room swarmed with tired people looking for places to sit.

It was enough to continue to hold down one chair, going on and on eating food he did not need.

Most of the people who passed through the other three chairs during the seventy minutes he sat had heard of Cotton's death. Two were discreet and said nothing about it; the others had asked for details. DeGraaf had inwardly groaned. Reluctantly, he told them a little bit more than they had known and quite a bit less than the police knew. He has always had a pretty good ability to guess which tidbits I like to keep to myself, so I suppose he didn't muck things up too badly. One of the people even volunteered to go back for more coffee, to which DeGraaf eagerly assented, as it made it possible to draw his vigil out longer.

By twelve-forty (two chicken sandwiches, a cheese sandwich, a bowl of chili and two cups of coffee later) it was obvious that Erikson was either not coming to lunch here at all or would arrive too late for DeGraaf. It was at least a ten-minute drive to the Cotton house. DeGraaf was annoyed that he had missed the man, but glad that he had not backed himself into trying to interview him in a crowded cafeteria with two interested spectators in the other seats. This ambivalence reconciled him to his failure. He decided that Erikson had sensibly concluded that the cafeteria would contain several hundred prying eyes and that he should therefore take a brown bag lunch to his office instead.

I arrived at the Cotton house before DeGraaf and, while waiting for him in my car out in front, asked myself several times why I had invited him. He wasn't the pathologist handling the body this time, nor did he have any other legitimate connection. Of course, I could take with me any "expert" I wanted. That was no problem. But why did I want him? I decided after some thought that it was principally his enthusiasm for the chase that did it. He was fun to have along—in his own annoying way.

When I saw his car pull up behind mine, I got out and we went into the house together. Melanie Cotton met us at the door at the same moment that the butler answered it. She ushered us in to see her aunt.

What a change from the night before! The little woman, her hair a fluffy bluish white, sat in a chair by the fire in the living room. At least I suppose it was the living room, although it was very long and narrow and dark with old oak and had as many books as the library. She looked up in a stately way as we entered, for all the world as if she had not heard the doorbell ring, or our voices, and as if she were surprised and delighted to see us. I noticed a slight smile on DeGraaf's lips. Melanie looked at her aunt with what seemed like clear-eyed understanding.

"Miss Cotton—Dr. Cotton—" I said, after the pleasantries, for I could not get used to this small, pretty woman as a pathologist, "I wish you would leave us with your aunt. It sometimes makes it easier for the person being interviewed to be alone with us."

She agreed and left.

"How upset that poor girl is," said Mrs. Spruance, the instant Melanie was gone. "Oh, please sit down. We're so disorganized here."

DeGraaf sat on a sofa and I on a straight chair.

"You were very shocked, I'm sure," I said, easing into it.

"Oh, of course, wouldn't you be? It was terrible."

"You appeared unusually upset."

She peered at me closely. "I *was* upset. My own brother! Killed right before my eyes like that. People are going to say such awful things."

"Right before your eyes? Could you tell me what it was you saw last night?"

"Why, Adam, of course. Dead. Just sitting there, dead."

"When do you mean?"

"When Dr. Coyne went over and spoke to him."

"Oh, not before?"

"What do you mean, before?"

"You said he was killed before your eyes. Did you mean you saw somebody kill him?"

"What a terrible idea! No, certainly not! I meant in the same room. Under our—our—in our presence, not actually under observation. Do you see?"

"I see," I sighed. My last hope that somebody had really noticed something was gone.

DeGraaf spoke up:

"Would you tell me about your brother?" he asked.

She looked at him, startled. "What about him?"

"Anything. What was he like? What did he do when he was home? That sort of thing."

"Oh." She looked as if the question were not any clearer to her. "Well, he read a great deal. And wrote. He published one professional article every year. And taxidermy. He stuffed animals. That's all I can think of."

"The animals he stuffed. Did he shoot them?"

"Yes, sometimes. He used to take hunting trips more than—well, as he got older he more often had friends send him game animals from their trips."

"I see."

"In dry ice, you know. Or sometimes in preservative. Sometimes just the skin."

"I see. How did he treat his employees?"

"Oh, there's nothing in that."

"In what?"

"They're awfully good people. They wouldn't do anything like that."

This all seemed pretty much of a hash, but DeGraaf went on with it, just as if it were profitable.

"What wouldn't they do?"

She answered coyly, "Oh, you know. Hurt Adam."

"Now, Mrs. Spruance, I only asked how he treated them. Certainly you can tell us that."

"Well, he was strict but fair. I know you must have heard about his firing Mr. Pryczyk. But he was entirely fair in doing so. He had warned him *very clearly* that the tulips should be planted thickly. They don't make much of a *show* if you string them out."

"Are you a gardener, Mrs. Spruance? You sound like it."

"Oh, I used to be, when Mr. Spruance and I had our own home," she said enthusiastically.

"Did you garden here some?"

"No. Well, no. Adam always said he paid the gardener and he wasn't going to have two people in the garden confusing each other. As a matter of fact, what he said was you don't keep a dog and bark yourself."

"In other words, he didn't allow you to garden?"

"That's right."

"Did this distress you?"

"Certainly not! It was his house. About the ser-

vants—Adam may have fired Pryczyk, but the butler and cook have been with Adam for many, many
years. All you had to do was please him. He was
very fair. I'm sure Johns will tell you that."

"Yes, he said something of the sort."

"You see?" She relaxed visibly.

"Can you tell me about his relationship with his
daughter?"

"Why he loved his daughter. And she was just
*devoted* to him. Her mother died when she was
very young, you know. I think Adam always wanted
a son, but naturally that was impossible after his
wife died. Melanie has been both a son and daughter to him. I just know that was why she went into
his profession—though why a pretty girl would
want to do pathology, I can't understand. I never
opposed her taking medical training. But I did think
something *nice* like pediatrics would have been a
better thing. Babies are so sweet."

"Yes, aren't they?"

"I've often thought she picked the specialty to be
even more of a son to her father, if you know what
I mean. Nothing peculiar about it, but just a desire
to take on masculine fields. Probably you'll think
I'm being silly. But these things do happen."

"I have no doubt."

"And she was always looking after him, like a
daughter, at the same time. What would he like to
drink after dinner, and could she help him with this
or that. Of course, I acted as housekeeper, so I took
a lot of details off her hands. And naturally she was
working too, so she couldn't very well be expected
to be home all the time dusting."

"I suppose the Johnses handled much of that."

"Oh, to some extent. But I had to see to the

menus, and plan meals and make sure things got done. Arrange for the window washers every spring and fall. Have the eaves cleaned. You know, there are a lot of details someone has to watch over in taking care of a house. I was always busy, I can tell you that."

"What was Adam's relationship with you?"

"He was my *brother*," she said, as if that were the answer to all things.

"Well, some sisters and brothers get along one way and some another. Could you characterize the relationship for us?"

"I don't see how," she said abruptly.

"Did you and Adam laugh over old times?"

"I don't remember doing so."

"Did you play games with him? Chess? Bridge? Checkers?"

"No."

DeGraaf turned to me. "Rob, I'm about through. Go ahead if you have anything else."

Anything else indeed! All the important questions had been left unasked.

"Mrs. Spruance," I said, "have you any definite memories about events last night before the body was found?"

"What do you mean? I felt odd all night. As if something were going to happen."

"Not that exactly. I mean, who got up from their chairs? Who walked around the room?"

"That very odd student from Arabia got up and *crept* about the room. Prowling, I would call it. I suppose he might have done it. Perhaps he was no good at his work and Adam was going to have him sent back home."

"Do you know that? Did Dr. Cotton say so?"

"No. Nobody said so in so many words. But the man looked strange."

"What else do you remember?"

"I believe that most of the guests got up to stretch their legs. You tend to do that when you're dummy, you know."

"Who got up?"

"I saw Dr. Coyne go to the refreshment table. Now let me see, who exactly was where? At our table Peter and that Mr. Passim—"

"Dr. Passim."

"If you say so. And at the other table Melanie and Alec and Mrs. Coyne. I believe I saw them all up. I don't remember seeing Dr. DeGraaf here get up, but he may have."

She mentioned DeGraaf's name with very little cordiality, indeed with stiffness, and I think she resented his asking her questions. Probably they struck her as not being proper behavior for a man who had been a guest in the house.

"And you?" I asked. "Did you get up?"

"No, I don't believe I did. I was tired. I work all day, keeping things going here. Fortunately, everyone went home early—oh, dear. I didn't mean—"

But what she didn't mean she couldn't say, either. She had been talking without thinking. She had moved glibly into stock phrases, and then suddenly remembered what had happened the night before. That was puzzling or maybe amazing. Could you lay it down to an extremely guilty conscience focused on something it was trying to keep secret, or to utter innocence?

DeGraaf had nothing more to say. In fact, he was staring off into the distance as if he did not even see the room we sat in. Which might have been just as well. I found the whole place gloomy. I thanked her and let her go. She said she appreciated that because she had so many things to do. "Arrangements" she called them.

DeGraaf had roused himself and been particularly gracious to her as she left, opening the door for her and thanking her for her frankness. He could have not been much more sickening if he had bowed and kissed her hand.

"Frank, huh?" I sneered when he came back and sat down.

"Well, everybody is allowed a few little lies, I'm sure. I feel sorry for her. Her lies are more interesting than the truth would have been."

"Oh? I don't rise to that bait any more. And all this courtesy. What are you trying to accomplish?"

"The same thing you are. Talking about sly behavior, if that's what you're trying to accuse me of, what about what you just did?"

"What?"

"You come into the lady's living room. She invites you to sit down. You proceed to ask her questions and when you're done, instead of leaving, *you* excuse *her* as if it were your office. And she buys it, poor thing, and thanks you for letting her go! Talk about gall!"

"All right. All right. You've made your point. Now that we're in possession here, what do you want to do with it?" Sometimes I humor him.

"Let's see who turns up." He told me what he had done so far that morning. Then he remembered an unresolved issue and said, "You haven't told me whether my prints were on the knife."

"No, they weren't. Naturally. But you knew that."

"Did I?"

"*Will you stop that!* What do you mean, did I?"

"Look at it this way, Rob. We have the following situation: somebody unknown came into the room without going through the windows or doors and stabbed an elderly man. Or, if you like it better, an invisible stranger came in through either the window or door, your choice, and stabbed an elderly man. Right? Now is that less amazing than the idea that my prints could be on a knife I'd never seen before?"

"That's silly. You can't *put* prints on a knife."

"Certainly you can. What if I had handled that knife at work, in the emergency room, say, and it had been carefully wrapped and brought here and used?"

"Umm. Possible. But not in this case."

"Why?"

"The prints weren't smeared. They were made by the *last* person to hold it."

"Fine. Okay, that makes it better. It was handled only while being used for the killing by a man or woman who was not in the room at the time. That's good."

"I didn't say it was good. I said that's the way it is. The prints are distributed over the knife in just the way you would leave 'em if you held it to push it into somebody's brain. The thumb print is on top, in such a position that it's clear the nail was pointing toward the blade. The four fingers are together on what would be the left side, tips pointing diagonally backward, just the way they would curl around a medium sized handle like that. And not only the fingertips show, but the insides of the fingers, and part of the palm. They slid forward slightly under the pressure of pushing it in, but the final impression is clear. Because of the longish blade, it penetrated a lot of brain. The only other prints on the knife are a few partly smeared ones of Cotton's. We got his from the body and his glass. They all match. Nobody could have handled that knife, certainly not to push it through bone, without messing those prints. It could not have been done with gloves over previous prints. Jeez! Give me some credit for intelligence."

"Oh, I do. I do." DeGraaf held his hand out as if he gripped a knife handle and turned it several ways, looking at the location of his fingers. I had already done that a dozen times, so I just watched. Then an idea hit me.

"Another reason why nobody could have planted a knife with prints already on it is that this knife was here. It was a part of the equipment."

"Right, Rob. That's very good."

"And if somebody had got the prints put on it, say, during the day and then left it on the table to use later in the evening, he couldn't be sure Cotton himself wouldn't handle it and mess everything up."

"Right! What about bringing in an exactly similar knife, with prints already on it, and just using it, then pocketing Cotton's?"

I hadn't thought of that, but the answer was obvious.

"Aside from the fact that he couldn't use it without smearing the prints, we know this knife is Cotton's because of his old prints on it."

"Okay. It was Cotton's knife. What about the

prints you took from the so-called suspects? Was there anything odd about any of them?"

"Strange you should ask that; there was."

"Go ahead."

"In one case the fingertips—maybe the whole hand, but we didn't print the whole hand—were so badly scarred that they don't really read as prints at all, but as odd flat areas and wrinkles."

"And who was it?"

"Dr. Peter Erikson."

# CHAPTER SIX

"Okay. Do what you can with that information," I said. "It certainly doesn't tell me anything."

"Me either. Unless you found 'odd flat areas and wrinkles' on the knife."

"We didn't," I said grumpily. I was irritated that when he had asked for a peculiarity, presto! there had been one. And contradictorily, I was annoyed that he couldn't make anything out of it. People are like that, and I don't pretend to be any better than the next man.

Then Melanie Cotton came into the room.

It was her house, of course, so there was no reason why she shouldn't, but I wondered whether she had been waiting outside the door and had heard any part of what we had said. Certainly she didn't allude to it.

"I was wondering whether you wanted to ask me anything else," she said.

She looked around for a place to sit and DeGraaf moved over to give her a place on the sofa. If his graciousness to the aunt had seemed spurious, his courtesy to Melanie looked perfectly genuine to me.

"Not really," he said, giving me no chance to say yes. "But I'm sure you have a lot of questions."

"Well, I have one," she answered and came out with the last one I would have expected. "Was Aunt Helen all right?"

"I thought you'd be worried," DeGraaf said. "She's very resilient, you know. And I think she's all right in your meaning, too."

"Oh, I'm glad. I get impatient with her sometimes. But I don't want her troubled. She hasn't done anything wrong. I suppose she hasn't done anything wrong in her whole life, poor thing. She means so well that—that I spent the whole morning trying to keep out of her way."

DeGraaf laughed, and Melanie, encouraged, blurted out everything that had happened in the house that morning.

"How did Aunt Helen get along with your father?" DeGraaf asked.

"Why, like brother and sister, I suppose."

"So she said, too. But Melanie, really, that won't do. I don't think it will hurt her to tell us the truth. Wasn't her panic last night due to her fear of him? Hadn't he threatened to turn her out? I heard him speak to her—how did it go?—she only had to oversee the housekeeping and she might at least have kept up a proper supply of wood. Something like that. The way he might speak to a careless employee?"

Melanie pressed her square little hands to her temples. "All right," she said after a couple of seconds. "I didn't want father to be painted in that way in your minds. He was sometimes authoritarian with people. I don't know why. Maybe he was very hurt by my mother's death. He suggested now and then that Aunt Helen wasn't doing her job. And I imagine Aunt Helen's first thoughts when she heard he was dead were that I would follow through on his last words on the subject. She has always believed that I hung on his every word, whereas in fact I have always been perfectly capable of disagreeing with him. She was being silly or panicky to think of it."

"His last words on the subject? Had they had a special blow-up yesterday?"

"Yes. No. Well, they had the same kind of thing from time to time. She had forgotten to call the painter in the morning, and he was very upset. But he would have gotten over it. After all, she was his sister."

"He threatened to turn her out?"

"How did I get into this discussion?" she grinned. "No. And that's the important point, too. He said he ought to turn her out. What that meant was that he wasn't going to. When he wanted to throw somebody out, he made it transparently clear."

"As he did with the gardener?"

"Yes. He said that and he meant that. But the gardener wasn't his sister."

"That's true." Gerritt was hesitating, looking at the girl—I mean woman—and I swear it was with tenderness, not suspicion. I had to admire her myself. She was courageous, and within the limits of honesty, she was trying to protect her aunt. I know I'm not supposed to feel that way. A policeman ought to grumble about anybody who does not rattle off everything he knows the first instant he is asked a question. Experienced policemen, however, know there isn't a soul who actually does this. Everybody hides something, if only the secrets of his inner character. A little honest frankness now and then is as much as I can expect.

Melanie sat waiting, small, but solid and competent rather than fragile, and appealing because she so obviously intended to cope with life. I cut into a silence that was not uncomfortable but wasn't getting us anywhere, either:

"Tell me about your gardener."

"Well, he worked for us about sixteen months, I think," she said.

"No tulip problem last spring?"

"Yes, but nothing to do with Mr. Pryczyk. The tulips that came up last spring were planted by the previous gardener the fall before. So, of course, they weren't Mr. Pryczyk's fault. My father took him out to see them in the spring and told him they were too far apart. And he said that when he—Pryczyk—planted the next batch this fall, they had to be close together or he'd have to let him go. I think that was fair warning, don't you?"

Fair it was, if not exactly generous or forgiving. I nodded, to help her. The girl seemed to alternate between trying to play down her father's unattractive side and trying to be frank when something came out into the light of day. In fact, I think she faced us out of a sense of obligation, for when a tap came at the door and Dr. Peter Erikson entered, the look in her eyes was not just one of happiness at seeing her fiancé. There was also a quality of relief.

"Would you like to talk with Peter?" Melanie asked. "Or maybe Alec?"

So Alec Spruance had stayed at the house as he

had said he would. I had wondered last night whether he might get nervous and go back to school. I wondered now if he had been detecting. Thinking of his short, sullen answers the night before, and the stranger he alone had seen, I quickly answered that I would like to talk with Alec. I say quickly because there was no telling whom DeGraaf might take a notion to ask for.

Peter Erikson took Melanie's hand protectively and they started out the door, only to run into Mrs. Spruance, who was reentering at a bobbing half-run.

"That man in the library—the policeman," Mrs. Spruance said to me breathlessly.

"Yes," I said.

"He wants to see you."

"Shall I tell Alec to come in here and wait?" Melanie asked.

"Yes, that'll be fine. I'll be right back."

DeGraaf and I went along to the library. Turgid was back on duty, replacing the night man.

"What's going on here, Turgid?" I said.

"Sir. Your orders were that I should not leave the premises unattended."

"So? I'm aware of what my orders were."

"Therefore I was required to send for you, sir. I thought you might want this information before you continued your interrogation of the present suspects."

"What information?"

"Approximately twenty minutes ago I unlocked the door—"

"Didn't I tell you to keep the door locked?"

"Yes, sir. But your intention was to prevent any person's effecting an unauthorized entrance. But as

I was present, such a thing was impossible. Am I wrong, sir?"

"Go on, go on."

"I was proceeding to unlock the door only because I had heard you enter the house, and in my estimation you would wish to examine the scene of the crime eventually. Naturally, your time is valuable, and it would delay you to a lesser degree if the door were unlocked—"

"Never mind that. What happened?"

"Yes, sir. Having unlocked the door, I continued in my previous pacing of the room. I engage in exercise to aid me in remaining alert." He paused here as if to give me a chance to say something unpleasant. Of course I did not. "I had proceeded to the farther side of the room, the north, when I heard the door creak."

"Yes, yes." Did the man want me to gouge the story out of him, piece by piece?

"Then, sir, I surmised that it was not you, because you would walk directly in. Therefore, I ceased to move and remained quietly in wait. This I concluded might be profitable, inasmuch as you might wish to know which member of the party had reason to wish to sneak in."

"Splendid."

"I continued to hold my breath. After a period I estimate as not exceeding six seconds, suggesting that the person outside may have been pausing to test whether he heard footsteps or other sounds from inside the room, the door proceeded to open. Would you care to guess who entered, sir?"

"Dr. Peter Erikson," said DeGraaf.

I had forgotten for the moment that DeGraaf was even in the room.

I'm glad to say I've never seen a man's chin fall so

far. Turgid had wanted to make me wait for it had he? He could have told me right away who had been sneaking into the room. Well, there was his comeuppance. I said coldly:

"You see, Turgid, there's no point in expecting your superiors not to know things. Would you describe what he did then?"

"Ah—I remained where I was to observe. Thinking the report might be useful," he added unnecessarily. "Being that I was on the far side of the room the said suspect may be presumed not to have detected me at the time in question."

"*Please*, Turgid," I said.

"Yes, sir. Dr. Erikson walked in. He moved softly and glanced about in a cautious manner, but as yet was unaware of my presence. He went towards the fireplace, still glancing about the premises, and then he saw me. Jumped."

"Erikson jumped? Or you did?"

"He did, sir. And then he endeavored to dissemble. Unskillfully, sir, in my estimation. Dr. Erikson said, and I quote verbatim, 'Oh, I'm glad you're here.' And I said, 'Yes?' He replied, 'I was afraid this room had been left open and anybody could get in. But since you're posted here, that's all right.' And he exited, closing the door after him, without another word."

This lack of prolixity must have surprised Turgid.

"This happened just now?"

"Oh, no, sir. Approximately four minutes ago."

DeGraaf said, "I imagine he was in here just before he came into the living room where we were talking with Melanie. Probably he often walks into the house without knocking. They've been engaged quite a while."

"Thank you, Turgid," I said. "You did the right

thing to wait a moment to see what he wanted. I wish he hadn't realized you were here that soon. He didn't take anything away, I suppose?"

"Oh, no, sir. I would never permit such a thing."

"Fine." I turned and walked out. I was glad to hear DeGraaf trailing along behind me. I had to admit that Alec Spruance seemed a little less promising now that we knew Erikson had been sneaking around looking for something, but I had to see Alec and I didn't want DeGraaf left behind messing things up. When we passed Erikson on our way to the living room, I said to him, "What were you looking for in the library, doctor?"

I heard a light choking sound from behind me, but DeGraaf didn't speak. Dr. Erikson said, "I wasn't actually looking *for* anything. I was looking in to see whether the room was guarded. I felt it should be. After all we don't—at least I don't—know what happened there last night. I didn't want to find something important missing later. Or something planted, for that matter."

"All right, Dr. Erikson, all right," I said. I could swear DeGraaf whispered behind me: "Serves you right."

Alec was waiting. In fact Erikson and Melanie had probably just come from settling him in the room. He was lolling unattractively in a chair under the head of a gazelle, his knees sticking out toward the windows, feet twisted under him, elbows splayed out over the arms of the chair, big hands hanging down toward his lap. It struck me that the ungainly stage that occurs in horses and deer at birth comes upon the human young about sixteen years late.

DeGraaf took the chair nearest Alec without looking at me, so I knew he had something on his mind and meant to have a hand in the questioning. Give DeGraaf an inch and he takes a mile. I looked grimly at the kid, hoping to impress him that it was time to tell the truth. At the same time I was backing into a chair, so DeGraaf got in the first question.

"Will you be staying here for a few days, Mr. Spruance?" he asked courteously.

That was all right. If he wanted to put the kid at ease, it was fine with me.

"Maybe. I've got to get back by Wednesday. We've got mid-terms." His tone was much less truculent than the night before. No telling why.

DeGraaf said, "You know, you're the only person who moves in and out of here, if you see what I mean. You don't live in the house permanently, but you see the family at intervals. So you'd see changes in things here better than they might. Also, you see them when they haven't got their company manners on. I could never hope to. In other words, you have a point of view that is unique and valuable. What can you tell me about them?"

The boy pulled himself a little more vertical.

"Them—all of them? Where do you want me to start?"

"Anywhere. Start with Adam, if you would. He's the center of this, surely. What are your observations about him?"

"Boy, he was a bastard, that's for sure."

"Can you be more specific?"

"Well, he tortured people. I'm not kidding," he added with a squeak to his voice, though neither of us had said a word. I suppose being taken seriously was an unusual experience for him.

"Go ahead," said DeGraaf.

"It's possible to torture people psychologically,

without ever touching them. Take my aunt. She isn't any bargain, of course. I guess you think I shouldn't say that, but she has never made any attempt to understand me. Well, she's been in this house—how long? Over twenty years! And in spite of that, he would still carry on as if any minute he wouldn't need her services any longer. Like, he'd ask kind of slyly, 'Do you have enough to do around this place, Helen?' And she'd turn pale and rush around the rest of the day shouting orders at the Johnses and dusting things and bumping into tables and making a lot of noise. And he'd just sit and sort of smile."

"I see what you mean. And I agree with your word, torture."

"Or if something didn't just please him—he'd let her have it. But quietly, you know? Like, uh— 'Can't the cook manage to get *fresh* salmon, Helen? It's the right time of year. The salmon run in May. After all, it's up to you to help her on things she doesn't understand. Or aren't you feeling up to it?' "

"What else?"

"Well, there were so many things. One time I was at dinner and heard them arguing. Melanie had written a paper opposing euthanasia for some journal. And you know how violent old Adam was about that! Thought people ought to be put out of the way. In my opinion, some cases should, but only—"

"What did Adam say about it?"

"Well, a lot. Said Melanie's article was published in an inferior journal. 'A journal of opinion,' he called it, not one of the factual research things. He had given Melanie examples of people who weren't expected to recover from coma but then had recovered, and she had used them in her article. But they hadn't."

"Hadn't what?"

"Hadn't recovered."

"That was a dirty trick."

"It sure was. He said he wanted to show her that she should check all sources. That was what he said. But I know that he just hated her point of view. His was always the only one. I think everybody is entitled to a point of view, don't you?"

"Certainly."

"He sure was a bastard. There was something else, too."

"What's that?"

"In my opinion, he resented that Melanie wasn't a boy. He resented the fact that he didn't have a son, and he sort of blamed Melanie. That's transference—unless it's displacement. It seems unreasonable, but it's a known psychological aberration."

"Yes, I'm sure. What did Melanie feel about this psychological aberration?"

The boy glanced at DeGraaf as if he suspected he might not be taken seriously. He saw nothing but interest on that bland face. He should only know DeGraaf as well as I do. At any rate, he answered, "Melanie was always nice to him. In my opinion, she had the other half of the problem. She tried to live up to his idea of a son, if you get me?"

"How did she do that?"

"Gee, it's obvious. She went into a masculine line of work. And old Adam's line besides, you see? Medicine. But even more so—pathology. And she always tried to talk shop with him. But she did daughter-type things for him, too. Bringing him his coffee. That sort of thing."

"You think Melanie was confused in her roles, then?"

He considered. "No, I wouldn't say that. Melanie is pretty strong-minded herself, if you ask me. For instance, she'd talk shop with him, right?"

"Right."

"But you see, she *wouldn't always agree* with him."

"I see."

"She'd take the other view and they'd debate the thing back and forth. It was kind of funny, because it would end with him pulling rank somehow, especially if he was losing. Either he'd say he had more experience than she had, or he was her father and knew better, or that was as much as he wanted to discuss about it. But if you ask me, Melanie wasn't often wrong."

"Did Adam resent that?"

"In my opinion, he never knew it. He thought he was always right."

"Yes. What about Peter Erikson? What do you think of him?"

"Oh, he's all right, I guess. He doesn't put a person down all the time. He's pretty nice."

"You sound like you're sort of lukewarm about him, though."

"It just seems he's such a goody-goody, you know? And he's too handsome. I don't trust anybody who's that handsome.

This was what I had felt, reduced to its bare bones. But it sounded so silly coming from him that I winced inwardly.

"What was his attitude toward Adam, or Adam's to him?" DeGraaf asked.

"Boy, it's really hard to say. Peter doesn't let *on*, you know. I mean, he'd even be nice to my aunt when she was having one of her foolish spells. I mean, he'd be nice to *any*body."

"What kind of foolish spells?"

"Oh, going around wiping her eyes and saying nobody liked her. Then Melanie would say that she liked her very much and not to be silly, everybody loved her. And Melanie and Peter would take her out to dinner someplace expensive. Then she'd feel better."

"I see. And what did Adam think of Peter?"

"He kind of sneered sometimes. But not much."

"How do you mean?"

"Well, I don't know exactly. Once or twice I heard old Adam say, 'That Peter Erikson's just an angel come to earth.' And in my opinion, Adam never said things to be really complimentary."

"No. I agree it sounds unlikely, given his character."

"But it didn't exactly *mean* anything, even backwards, if you see what I mean."

At this indecisive point, I had to break in.

"If you people are done gossipping," I said, "I'd like to find out a few things."

"Sure," said DeGraaf.

The kid looked like he had forgotten I was there.

"About this intruder you saw last night—"

"I didn't see any intruder."

"Now, listen! You're not going to pull that on me. You said you saw somebody come into the room last night. And not any of the card players. You're going to back down on that now, are you?" I may have become a little upset.

"No, I'm not. But I didn't say I'd seen any *intruder*."

The kid was getting impudent. Meanwhile, there was DeGraff, staring at the head of a lynx and sitting with his arms folded in that particular way that means you want to dissociate yourself from what's going on.

I said, "You'd better explain."

"But it was perfectly clear. I thought I saw somebody come in while we were playing. I wasn't so interested in the game as all that, and if nobody else saw him, maybe it's because they all take these games so seriously."

A teenager talking about taking things seriously! But what was I to do? I just stared at him. He felt the silence after a few seconds and went on talking.

"I never said it was an intruder. In my opinion someone came in from outside the room. But that could have been Johns, and Johns isn't an intruder. I didn't look at him closely. I just saw him out of the corner of my right eye. You know what I mean."

"I'm working on it. Tell me your best guess."

"That's it. That's all I can think of."

"Man or woman?"

"I guess a man. It would be more unusual if it were a woman, wouldn't it? Unless it was Mrs. Johns."

"Well, was it Mrs. Johns?"

"I don't know. You're being very silly, Inspector. I've already told you I didn't especially look. And now you want to know whether I think it was Mrs. Johns! It could even have been somebody from the other table."

"You're saying you wouldn't rule out *any* sort of person?"

"Well, I guess if it had been the circus tall man or a person wearing a gorilla suit I would have looked twice, wouldn't I?"

"I couldn't tell you. I suppose we can say you think you saw somebody not too unusual who may or may not have been somebody already in the room. That's a big help, son."

"That's what I get for trying not to imagine things."

DeGraaf broke in. "We're very grateful to you for not embellishing, Mr. Spruance. You would be amazed how many people do add details they think they *should* have seen. Can you tell us your personal observations of Mr. Johns, Mrs. Johns, or Mr. Pryczyk?"

"Oh, yeah, the gardener was mad at Adam. But you must know that. I haven't seen him much, though. I've been away at school and when I'm here in the evenings, Pryczyk has gone home. The Johnses have been here for years and years, though. They get along. They're very quiet. If you ask me, they were used to old Adam. In fact, if you ask me, I bet they were more put out by Aunt Helen fussing around than they were by old Adam and his orders."

"In what way?"

"They were sort of professional about it. They'd take one of old Adam's orders, and they'd just *do* it, don't you see? But Aunt Helen was always suggesting one thing and then changing her mind. Because she was so insecure, you know. And then she'd reverse herself back again, and all. I think they just went ahead their way and figured she'd agree with what they did after it was done. Of course, Aunt Helen was always talking as if she did all the work. In fact, if old Adam gave Aunt Helen room and board to act as a sort of housekeeper, I wouldn't say, in my opinion, he got his money's worth."

About five minutes later, having gotten rid of the kid, I said to DeGraaf, "We've been playing around with these people long enough. In *my* opinion, it's time to check into that business of Johns and Pryczyk in the hall. Either their story holds up, in which case I don't know what the hell we're going to do, or it doesn't hold. And then either they did it, or they let somebody else do it, or they don't want to admit they weren't watching all that time."

"Now why would they not want to admit that? It wasn't their job to guard the door."

"I don't know why. I'm only being thorough. So that you won't remind me that the third logical possibility exists."

"Don't get defensive. I'll tell you one thing. They were on that bench a part of the time, anyhow."

"How do you know?"

"There's a fair amount of dried mud—little pieces that might fall off a boot—around one end of the bench."

I was annoyed. Turgid was going to hear about this. "It could have been there for days."

"In *this* house? With company expected? Why, there isn't even any dust on the tops of the doors. Try them. That hall would have been spotless at the moment the guests arrived. I bet the mud wouldn't be there today, either, except that Mrs. Johns' cleaning schedule must have been thrown off by events."

"I still say you can't be sure when the mud fell off the shoes."

"No one sat there after the body was found. There was a lot of walking back and forth, but no sitting in the hall. The mud that is under the bench was made by someone sitting with his feet stuck back. Some of the guests may have worn muddy rubbers, but these are little V-shapes that look like they fell from between the corrugations of work boots. And none of the guests wore work boots."

"We'll have to be sure."

"Then *get* sure. It shouldn't be any problem matching the mud to the boots; they're as good as a mold."

"And anyway, Johns and the gardener could have sat there discussing how they were going to commit murder."

"Somehow, Rob, I think that if you're going to commit a murder, you don't sit outside the door talking about it. It's not that you'd be afraid of being heard. The doors in this house are too thick for that. It's that psychologically you'd want to put yourself at some distance while you talked it over. Then you'd creep back and do it."

"Maybe."

"And anyway, why sit *there?* Why should the two of them get together to swear that nobody had gone into the room? If they were involved in the murder, they should claim to have been together *somewhere else* for all of that period of time, so that almost anybody could have killed Adam. It doesn't make any sense for them to put themselves in this ambiguous position unless it's true. I've been inclined to believe them from the first, without even talking to them."

"Maybe they sat there while somebody else did it —the man whose fingerprints are on the knife."

"*Three* people in it together? Do you really think so?"

"It's happened before."

"Oh, *everything* has happened before. But some things are extremely improbable, given the people and the situation."

"A man could have come in planning to murder

Cotton, a man they didn't know. But since they both have grudges against Cotton, they let him get away with it."

"Oh, sure. Rob, you're getting desperate, not that I don't sympathize. What did this man do? Walk up to the door and say, 'Gentlemen, I'd like to kill your boss. Will you stand guard for me a minute or two?' Why should he trust them? What's to stop them from calling the police as soon as he's finished, so that all this awkward suspicion wouldn't fall on them?"

"Say! Maybe they hired him."

"Pryczyk wasn't fired until late yesterday afternoon. He didn't have time to hire a killer. They're not exactly flooding the marketplace. 'One killer, size small enough to be almost invisible.' Second, the butler and the gardener do not have that kind of money. Third, no professional killer is going to put his future completely in two other men's hands by walking in and doing a murder practically before their eyes."

"Listen, Gerritt, we have a murderer who was willing to walk in and do it practically before the eyes of *eight* other people."

That shut him up for a minute.

"Oh, all right," he said. "I think, logically, the story the butler and gardener tell has to be true. But let's be sure. Let's go give the Johnses the once-over."

"Once-over," I said, "is an outmoded expression."

Mrs. Johns was in the kitchen. Since we had asked her husband to find her for us, he rather naturally trailed along behind. I was just debating whether to let him stay, when DeGraaf, taking a lot on himself as usual, said, "Mr. Johns, please sit down. I want Mrs. Johns to realize we aren't here to distress her."

The lady in question had been doing something aggressive to a large fish. "Oh, I'm sure of that, sir," she said calmly, wiping her hands after putting the fish in a long pan.

"And I'll just sit on the table here, if you don't mind," DeGraaf went on. Under the circumstances, this is no social call, but we can be comfortable. Let's see, how about the other chair for the minion of the law?"

His idea of putting people at ease is not mine, but I took the chair. Johns, seeing that sitting was the order of the day, sat on the wood box, so erect that he still looked as if he were on duty.

"We both understand you have questions to ask," said Mrs. Johns, entirely on her own. "It was a terrible thing to have happen, and the sooner it's cleared up, the better." It sounded a bit like she was talking about spilled custard. "This isn't that sort of house. We've never even had a burglary."

"I check every lock every night," said Johns.

"And everything has always been done very properly," Mrs. Johns said, in summary. I had the feeling that she did not know quite what propriety had to do with murder, but wanted to make it clear that she worked in a respectable house. I half expected DeGraaf to console her by saying that these things could happen in the best of families.

"Would you say it was a happy house, Mrs. Johns?" he asked.

For the first time the lady paused before speaking. "I don't—well, I suppose it wasn't always very jolly," she said reluctantly. We both waited. "Dr. Cotton never allowed a lot of noise, not even when

Miss Melanie was young. I don't really know quite what to say. Did you know him, sir? You were invited last night, so we rather thought you must have."

"Yes, but not well."

"But you must have heard about him, to know what he was like." She was reluctant to criticize her employer directly.

"Yes, I suppose I did, Mrs. Johns. How exactly did you cope with him?"

She laughed a little at that. Her behavior was certain to convince DeGraaf she was telling the truth. I wasn't so sure.

"We coped with him the simplest way, sir. We did what he asked."

"Did you like him?"

"Well, now, you could say I didn't mind him. You understand, I was being paid to cope with him. I felt sorry for Miss Melanie and Mrs. Spruance sometimes. After all, if we had found our situation impossible, we could easily have found another job. But naturally, they couldn't."

"Yes, I see what you mean."

DeGraaf was sitting there looking owlish, obviously willing to go on chatting with the Johnses all day. But I'd gotten to the point where I couldn't stand it any longer. Face it—this was the day after the murder, and I didn't even know which way to look. I said, "Do you have anything else to ask, Gerritt, or may I also ask a few things?" He just smiled and nodded toward the Johnses, which meant that I could go ahead. Nice of him.

"All right," I said, "you realize everybody is a suspect until we get to the bottom of this." I was a little sorry about the way that came out. It sounded like a bad movie. But DeGraaf said nothing at all and both the butler and his wife looked innocently at me. "Mrs. Johns, did you see your husband and Bart Pryczyk sitting in the hall last night?"

"Yes, I certainly did. I went out after I had the first load in the dishwasher, because I couldn't imagine what was keeping him so long. He had set out all the glasses and taken in the ice long before. And there they were, on that bench."

"What did you do?"

"Do? I didn't want to disturb them. I thought my husband had done quite a good job of calming Mr. Pryczyk down. He's an excitable person. So I didn't want to break their mood, you see, with Mr. Pryczyk talking more sensibly. I just went and made them some tea. It seemed all right to leave them there, because the bridge games would go on quite a while."

"How do you mean, 'all right?' "

"Dr. Cotton would not have wanted the guests to find the servants there, in the hall, drinking tea," she said without rancor. "But as nobody would be apt to come out, I thought it was safe enough. They would just get up and leave if they heard any stirring around inside the library."

"In other words, they were keeping doubly careful watch on the door because they didn't want to be caught there?"

"Yes, sir."

"Mrs. Johns, how long have you known Bart Pryczyk?"

"Why, I think about a year now. No. A little more. Since he came to work here."

"And not before that?"

"No. Except technically—I let him in the day he came for an interview, about a week before he took the job."

"And you, Johns?"

"The same, sir. Except that I did not see him when he came for the interview. I was away that day. That was how Mrs. Johns happened to be answering the door."

"Where were you?"

"At the dentist."

Somehow it had never occurred to me that butlers went to dentists. But of course, they must.

"If we had information," I said, "that you had known Pryczyk before—"

"That would be impossible, sir," Johns said flatly. "We simply didn't. Not until he came here."

"Where did Cotton get him?"

"Wolf and Lambert's employment agency, sir. It's the one he always used."

"Got you two there, did he?"

"Oh, no, sir. Wolf and Lambert's wasn't in existence back then. No, we came through a recommendation from a friend."

"Hmmm. Who?"

"A Dr. Gerretson, for whom we worked for three years. He was at Hastings General. Eye surgery. An elderly man, sir. At the same time he decided to move to a retirement home in Florida, Dr. Cotton was looking for a couple. It was just after Mrs. Cotton had died, and he had the house to be looked after and little Melanie, as she was then. Dr. Gerretson very kindly suggested that we would do."

"I see." For some reason, I had the feeling that DeGraaf wanted to catch my eye. I glanced at him. Maybe I was imagining things, for he just looked utterly blank—still, you have to know him a while before you distinguish between his wide variety of blank looks, and this seemed to be the kind he reserved for people who were just too plausible. I went on with my own train of thought:

"And you've been here ever since?"

"Oh, yes, sir," said Mrs. Johns. "Twenty-four years."

"No fights? No disagreements?"

"No, sir."

DeGraaf was right. They were just too bland, too readily smooth in their answers. It suggested an attempt to hide something. "Do you realize," I said, "how unbelievable that is?" She stared at me. "Here is a man everybody considered difficult. Grouchy. Even nasty, to hear them tell it. And you're in the house with him twenty-four years and never a cross word? You don't think I'm going to buy that?"

"You see, sir—" she began, but her husband was talking too.

"It's very much as Mary Ellen explained before, sir," Johns said. "We took a professional attitude toward our job, and toward Dr. Cotton. Much as a physician does, you see. If your doctor had to give you an injection, he might not like causing you pain, and he might wish to avoid the disagreeableness. But it would do you good, and it would be what he was paid to do. So he disregards aspects that a non-professional would find emotional, if you understand me. We have a very unemotional attitude toward our job, sir. We give the service we're paid to give."

"Well, that's very neatly put, Johns."

"After all, sir," he said without a blush, "I've had many years to consider the position."

I imagine he thought he was one up on me there. DeGraaf added, "Probably wouldn't have lasted twenty-four years with any other attitude."

"Can you give me Bart Pryczyk's address?" I asked Johns.

"25 East Irving Park," he said.

"Thank you, Johns. Mrs. Johns. I think that'll do it for today." To DeGraaf I said as we went down the hall, "Let's see this Pryczyk. That'll probably be the end of it right there."

"I should think *so*," he said.

"I mean they must have let somebody slip past them."

"And I mean they didn't."

"You'll see."

"And you were the one who had an alternative. That they were in cahoots."

"One or the other."

"Sloppy, Rob. Very sloppy."

Melanie Cotton was standing near the front door with Peter Erikson as we approached. They were not touching hands as they had been before. This did not necessarily mean that they'd had a falling out, of course.

DeGraaf said, "We're just leaving. I hope we can talk with you soon, Dr. Erikson. You two would probably just as soon cheer each other up right now, though."

"Certainly," said Dr. Erikson, somewhat tonelessly.

"I'll try to catch you at the hospital."

I nodded at both of them and we let ourselves out. They stood watching us, not saying a word.

A moment of misgiving assailed me. "Gerritt," I said, "don't you have to be at work?"

"I have today and tomorrow off in Emergency. I've been working weekends lately."

Pryczyk's apartment was in one of those squat

buildings with three and a half floors, just short enough so that the landlord did not have to provide an elevator. Tired and worn out, all the colors of the place seemed to have run together to make a mud shade. The blocks of which the place had been constructed were a gray concrete, browned with age. The carpeting in the ground floor entry was a pattern of flowers, once in color, but age and half-hearted cleaning had discouraged it, and it was now a mix of grayish brown, brownish gray, tannish brown and grayish tan. Even the narrow windows that let squeezed, thin beams of light into the entry were yellowed with grime. The owner had decided that a yellow, sixty-watt bulb was good enough for the hall.

I had half expected Pryczyk to be out looking for a job. This would have been fine with me, since a few words with his wife alone might have been just as revealing as having him repeat what he told Lem last night. I don't like to call first to see who's home because I don't like rehearsed answers. Anyway, Pryczyk himself answered the door, and that took care of that.

Before I even announced our names, he knew what we were there for. He walked us into a tiny living room and sat us on a grayish tan couch. A relative of the entry carpet, slightly less worn, lay on the floor, this one with the distinction of having some grayish green patches still visible. Pryczyk's wife had tried to deal with the dun-colored drabness of the place. There were two needlepoint pillows on the couch, one of a peacock in blues and greens so alive I wished I owned it myself. She had thrown a green and yellow knitted afghan over the upholstered chair. Under it, I guessed was brownish gray fabric. The effect was more gallant and cheerful than complete, but she had tried.

She came in herself a few seconds after we had sat down. She had short brown hair worn loosely curled, and was enormously pregnant. She wore a gigantic face-the-facts yellow tent; her arms and legs looked fragile in comparison with the middle section that had taken her over. I liked her at once. I think DeGraaf did too, for he smiled and nodded at her as Pryczyk introduced us. Her name was Susan, and she insisted on perching on the arm of the afghan-covered chair while her husband sat in it. Her husband said no, that she would sit in it and he stand. She told him that she would feel better on the arm and he sat. I imagine it was easier for her to perch than to fold. As he sat, the chair sagged. Its springs were shot.

"We don't intend to worry you," said DeGraaf, giving himself a spurious official position by hogging the conversation. "We have to get as many facts as possible about everybody, you know, but we haven't any desire to upset you."

"Oh, I don't upset too easily," she said lightly, and she smiled at us.

"Damn good thing she doesn't, too," Bart Pryczyk said, in a far tenser tone than his wife's. "Here we are, Suzy eight months pregnant, and I'm out of a job. Cotton was a bastard if I ever saw one."

"Bart, don't," said his wife. "The man's dead."

"And unmissed, I'll bet." He turned back to us. "I guess Suzy thinks you'll jump to the conclusion that I killed him because I'm mad at him. Personally, I'd be willing to bet that half the people who knew him didn't like him. I'm not alone in that, and I'm not going to hide what I think."

His wife sighed, but did not interrupt.

"We've heard he was hard to get along with,"

said DeGraaf. Pryczyk snorted at this woeful under-statement. "What made you take the job in the first place?" DeGraaf asked.

"I needed it. We have to eat."

"But seriously—there are always *some* other jobs."

"Okay. Yes, there are. But I'm not trained for most of them. I'm not a mechanic; I don't type; I don't punch computer cards. What I do know is gardening. My father was an estate gardener. And I like it, too. There aren't many gardens like Cotton's in the city. You get outdoors and you putter around with growing things. It's almost like being in the country."

"Why don't you get a job in the country?"

"There aren't many of those jobs left. In the old days a person like me could be head gardener at a big estate, and he might have an apartment over the garage or coach house where he and his wife could live. But now the big estates have mostly sold off their extra land. People don't want huge live-in staffs. They've either sold their garages and coach houses or they rent them to bring in extra cash. They want somebody to come in by the day. And then you've got a long commute to get there. I don't know. Maybe that would have been better. But you know, spending over an hour getting to work isn't good either. Everything seems so difficult these days."

His wife sat quietly, looking down at him. She would be very tactful, I thought, at dealing with the depression of a man out of work. We had our own problems.

"What about this business about the tulips that Cotton fired you over? Was it an excuse?"

"No, it was real. The old bastard wanted the damn things just a couple of inches apart."

"And you refused?"

"Well, you know, it isn't right. My father always said they lasted longer if they were six inches apart. And that's the way we always did them."

"But what did it matter?"

"Tulips decline," he said patiently, as if he were talking to a child. "The first year you put them in, they are the biggest. The next year the flowers are a little smaller. Of course, you can replant them every year. A lot of the public displays do that, and that was what Cotton wanted to do, but it's wasteful. What you want to do is work some bone meal into the bed when you first put them in, to give them something to keep them up, you know? Then give them about six inches between bulbs so they all will get enough food and water, and then they don't decline as fast. Why, you can keep a bed at its peak sometimes *five years* if you handle it properly."

"Cotton," I said, "didn't want that?"

"No. He wanted to just shove 'em in, use 'em up, and replace them."

"But why did it matter to you?" I asked. "It was his yard."

Pryczyk looked at me sadly. "It was my responsibility," he said.

"I can understand that," said DeGraaf. "Mr. Pryczyk is a gardener, not a janitor. He doesn't just shove in bulbs. He's a craftsman and he was trained to do it right."

Pryczyk nodded at DeGraaf and actually smiled. When he wasn't being sullen, he looked much more intelligent.

"So how long have you known the Johnses?" I asked.

"What? Oh, the butler and his wife? Just since I got there. I think I met Mrs. Johns first when I went in for the interview. I don't exactly remember."

"Not before that?"

"No. Of course not. What are you trying to prove?"

"I'm trying to find out, not prove. How did you two happen to be sitting in the hall while the bridge party was going on?"

"I told your policeman all that stuff."

"Tell me again. I haven't heard it from you, and you might remember something else."

He shot me a rebellious look, but his wife had her hand resting softly on his arm and he took a breath instead of shouting.

"Cotton had just given me notice that afternoon," he said.

"So?"

"Well, I had been carrying in some stuff that was kept in a little room off the front hall. Tools. So there I was. I was mad, and I ran into Johns as he was coming out of the library after supplying them something or other. The ice, I think."

"When was that?"

"About nine."

"Why were you still at work so late?"

"I was finishing up. Putting everything away. After all, he'd fired me."

"Oh. Okay. Go on."

"I guess I said something like, 'What a nasty bastard!' to Johns. He knew I had been upset all evening, anyway. Well, they couldn't hear us from inside the library. You can't hear anything through the doors in that place. So Johns just sat down with me to talk."

"Right on the bench in the hall?"

"Yup. That was where we were, so that was where we sat."

"How long did you stay there?"

"We were still there when all the fuss started."

"You mean calling the police and all that?"

"Yes. Well, when we heard everybody shuffling around inside we got up. We didn't want Cotton to find us there."

"You expect me to believe that you and Johns sat there *all* the time they were playing. Two hours or something like that?"

"We did. That's all. I have to admit that Johns is a sympathetic person. He seemed to care about it, really. He tried to tell me Cotton was being fair by his own standards. Having warned me, you know? I didn't really buy that. It didn't make Cotton less of a bastard. I don't tell him how to do his surgery. But Johns was trying to be nice. He said he knew of some people who might need a gardener. Somebody with a big place far west of town. And he said he'd give me a recommendation himself, if I wanted. He knew we were expecting a baby. He's sympathetic about babies, I guess. Mrs. Johns even brought us a mug of tea at one point."

I sighed. "Couldn't you have gone into the kitchen to talk? Wouldn't it have been more comfortable?"

"I don't know about comfortable. The hall bench is upholstered. Old Cotton only allowed wood straight chairs in the kitchen. He didn't want the help lolling around ignoring their work, I'll bet. He was a real bastard."

"All right. All right."

"He told me—Johns, that is—there wasn't any point in harboring a grudge. He said all the things everybody always says when something like this happens."

Susan Pryczyk looked at the ceiling as he made

this remark, but still she didn't speak.

"But he meant it well," Pryczyk went on. "And I felt like sitting. I'd been working hard all day. And then when you're suddenly fired and you get angry, and what with packing up all the tools and going around for hours wanting to sock him one—"

He stopped. DeGraaf said, "Exactly. You get worked up and the emotion tires you out. And then when you sit down and somebody is sympathetic, the exhaustion catches up with you."

I thought to myself I didn't need DeGraaf helping the man flesh out his story.

"Mrs. Pryczyk," I said, "did *you* ever know the Johnses before this?"

"No. Actually, I've never met them. Dr. Cotton didn't encourage Bart to bring me to work with him or anything like that." She looked so completely open-eyed that I decided not to ask her anything else. I asked Pryczyk to lend me the boots he had been wearing the night before, though. It appeared he had them on. Looking sullenly at me, he changed to a pair of shoes and handed me the boots. Mrs. Pryczyk went into the kitchenette and found a brown bag for them. Meanwhile, I asked Pryczyk for the names of his previous employers. He wrote them down with my pen on my pad. There weren't many. He had worked five years for a neighbor of the man to whom his father had been head gardener. This was in Barrington. And he worked for a short while for the city, trimming trees on the parkway, a job he said he didn't like. That was about the time of his marriage.

We said goodbye to them and left.

Halfway to the car, I turned to DeGraaf.

"Do you realize," I said, "we forgot to ask him

whether he saw anybody go into the library while he and Johns were sitting in the hall?"

"You forgot. I didn't."

"Well, I didn't hear you ask him."

"I didn't ask him. I just said I didn't forget. I didn't need to ask. He and Johns both told your man last night that nobody passed them. Nobody went into that room."

"We can't be sure of that."

"Do you think he's going to remember an assassin with a bushy black beard and Malay kris today, just because we came here, when he didn't last night? He was just as wide awake and sober then as he is now."

"He might. To cover up that he and Johns killed the old man."

"You're kidding. He'd have 'remembered' last night if that were the case."

"People can be stupid. And I'm not kidding. Johns may have a grudge against Cotton we don't know about. Pryczyk has one we do know about. One did it and left the other on guard in the passage. They admitted they were there in case somebody saw them."

"One of them sneaked in and the door didn't squeak?"

"You people were concentrating on what you were doing. You didn't hear it. Maybe a truck went by in the street at the same minute, or a plane overhead."

"And elderly, respectable Johns put his life in the hands of Pryczyk from that moment on?"

"Well, having done it, each had something on the other. That ought to keep each in line, from the other one's point of view."

"Have you ever heard of squealing to get a reduced sentence?"

"Gerritt, they'd have no reason to break up. There isn't any money for them to fight over, as far as we know. You're just being stubborn and resisting the obvious."

"I don't think they're involved in any sort of collusion. Last night I thought it was very unlikely in terms of logic. Today, having seen both of them in home settings, I think it's also impossible from the psychological angle. You're going round and round with this, thinking about ways they *might* have done it and patching up the leaks. But it won't work. We've got to take the blocked passage as a given and break out of that whole line of thought."

"Oh, yeah?"

"And besides, you're forgetting something."

"What?"

"The reason you were so eager to find something wrong with the testimony Johns and Pryczyk gave us. The fingerprints on the scalpel aren't Johns' or Pryczyk's either. You still have to work another hand into the equation."

Well, that was all right to say. But I knew from experience that if you have a hothead like Pryczyk in a case, you start there to look for your answer.

We walked on past the car, because we were annoyed with each other. DeGraaf thought I was being unimaginative and I thought he was being pig-headed, and we didn't want to leave it that way.

We kept walking until we came to Grogan's Chinese Rathskeller, which isn't a bad place to eat if you like pizza, and by unspoken agreement we turned in the door and sat in a booth. DeGraaf ordered a sixteen inch anchovy pizza without asking me. He does things like that now and then—things you'd think were done out of arrogance. But my guess was that he remembered the last time we had ordered pizza, three years before, I had ordered anchovy.

"You realize," he said, as if we were in the middle of a conversation, "how much easier it was for anybody *in* the room to kill Cotton than for anybody to come in from outside and do it. An insider would know whether all the bridge players were sitting down and engrossed and so on. An insider could walk around for a few minutes without making anyone suspicious. No one who came in from outside would have the same opportunity to bide his time like that."

"Sure. Except they used another person's arm to strike the blow."

I wanted to be conciliatory. But it was obvious that someone had come into that room. We both sat drinking beer. DeGraaf said 'wow' under his breath.

I said, "We've got to look into the question of those windows. One of them was open, remember?"

"Robert, I was *facing* the windows. Nobody came in that way."

"You know that. I don't know that."

He gave me a pitying glance but forebore to say that I didn't trust his good sense or alertness—which would have been a fair retort to make.

"You had one of your minions looking over the ground outside the window. I saw him," he said.

"Yeah."

"I assume, since you haven't said anything about it, that he didn't find anything suspicious?"

"Yeah. But there's grass underneath the window. He might not."

"No footprints, I suppose. But were there trampled areas? Broken grass blades? That kind of thing?"

"No."

DeGraaf paused a second, then, as if he couldn't help himself, he rubbed his hands together rapidly, palm to palm, like a man trying to contain his enthusiasm and not quite managing. I'd seen him do it before when sheer zest overcame him.

"Don't you see how fantastic this is, Robert?" he said.

"What do you mean? No, I don't. A man has been killed, and I have a job that makes me responsible for finding out who killed him. And I'm just not anywhere near proving anything."

"You know, that's very revealing. You say you're not near to *proving* it. I say you're not near to guessing even how it was done—let alone proving it. We have a murder apparently committed by a man or woman who could not have been in the room. How did he do it? How did he reach past all the people watching? And then how did he get out again?"

"The butler and gardener let somebody slip past because they hated Cotton."

"The easiest solution, in fact."

"What do you mean? It appears to be the most probable."

"No, it isn't. In fact, they're all improbable. I can take every person in the room, every person in the house, and every outsider, for that matter, and for every one of them it's *very improbable* he or she ever killed Cotton."

He was nearly jumping out of his seat with enthusiasm.

"Well, Cotton's as dead as he's ever going to get," I said, as sourly as I could.

"Of course. But think of it this way: if I had come to you twenty years ago and described the sequence of events that were going to lead up to this murder, through all of Cotton's life, you'd tell me it was all very, very unlikely to happen."

"No doubt. Murder is uncommon. What of it?"

"Rob, that isn't the point. It's true for anything. That's what's so nice about life; it's all so improbable. Where were you born, for instance?"

"In Chicago."

"In Chicago. All right. Now look at it this way. There are thousands and thousands of towns and cities in the world. Isn't it improbable, *vastly* improbable, that you would happen to be born in Chicago?"

"Well, my mother happened to be here at the time."

He looked at me with sorrow. "Also improbable. And your gene combination—extremely improbable."

"But look, Gerritt. You're not making any sense. After all, the world is here and we all have to be someplace."

"Certainly. We have an entire world of stuff— and all of it fantastically improbable. That's why it's all so damned interesting!"

I sighed. It was not interesting. In fact, when we finally got to the explanation of what had caused the murder, it was more likely to be sordid. Amateurs are simply too romantic. The essential quality for doing my job well is hard-headedness.

"You are the person," I said, "who is always telling me to boil down the possibilities in a murder investigation until I get to the most probable person."

He stared at me. "Where do you see a contradiction, Robert? You go through all the people involved, all their unlikely interests and their wild ideas—except that *you* regard them all as just normal, dull variations on the human species. But never mind that. Then of all the wildly unlikely, fleight-of-fancy, fascinating things that might have been true about this one or that one, you pick the one that, of all those remote possibilities, is the least improbable. And the least improbable is, of course, the most probable."

I was annoyed with him now. "Oh, well, if that's all! It's just a different way of saying the same thing."

"No, it isn't really, you know. It's a different way of looking at life. And that makes all the difference."

This was as close to an argument as we had had in the case. He knew it and stopped there, picking up another piece of pizza. How that man can eat! I was feeling insulted, because I believed that my ability to enjoy life was being questioned. I couldn't resist snarling one more remark.

"Well, this murder isn't improbable," I said. "It's impossible."

"Hooray," he said.

# CHAPTER SEVEN

The body was released that same evening to a funeral home. The autopsy had shown nothing beyond the obvious. The knife blow to the brain had caused death, had been the only cause of death, and had killed as nearly instantly as possible. In addition, the knife, plunging through the center of the brain, severed the connection between brain and the organs of speech. Therefore, even before the heart stopped beating, the only sound would have been an escape of air from the sagging lungs. There would have been no cry for help.

DeGraaf, though a pathologist, did not do the autopsy. For one thing, since he was in the room at the time of the attack, he was technically a suspect. Secondly, there was nothing about the manner of death that required his expertise. Mostly they call him in now only for the unusual cases.

Melanie Cotton, of course, did not see or do the autopsy either, though she planned to go back to work the next day, immediately after the funeral. Melanie alone, or Melanie and her aunt, had decided to have the funeral the morning after the body was released. I suspect Aunt Helen considered this to be indecent haste, but Melanie must have convinced her that the sooner the formalities were over the sooner the publicity and the gossip would die down. Also, they scheduled the funeral for very early in the morning—eight o'clock—hoping that very few of the idle curious would turn up at that hour. Their own friends and Cotton's old friends, mostly physicians, were well used to rising at six or earlier, and any of them who wanted to come were welcome. Melanie, I believe, telephoned those she felt would really want to know.

It was cold and windy the morning of the funeral. As a matter of fact it was still quite dark—one of those mornings when you are not quite sure whether the sun has risen because of impenetrable clouds. We stood, DeGraaf and I, in front of the Episcopal church, me shivering and DeGraaf looking around and sniffing the air like a bird dog. The service had been short, thank heaven, and we were about to go to the cemetery.

Melanie came out of the church looking pinched and cold. She came directly to us, with a glance at the other mourners. She wanted to explain why there were so few.

"There weren't a lot of people I felt I should call," she said. "He'd fought with quite a number of his old friends." She glanced at the hearse, then at the casket as it was borne from the church. "Several of them came. It was good of them—"

Cotton's lawyer was there, and a couple of nurses who had worked with him for years in surgery. Apart from three older doctors and their wives, only the people who had been at the bridge game

Sunday night had come, and the family, and the Johnses. Mrs. Johns was actually crying. The Coynes had come more out of having been present the night he was killed than because of any long-term friendship. Passim, too, I suppose; he stood shivering outside the church in the April wind off the lake. Young Alec leaned from one foot to the other, all the time maintaining that attitude peculiar to persons in their late teens at adult ceremonial functions. I can best describe it as a condescending tolerance. He looked away from any of the accouterments of mourning, folded his arms, and generally disassociated himself. Mrs. Spruance, on the other hand, was determined to view the presence of anybody at all at the funeral as a specific tribute to Adam Cotton himself, which was absurd. She carried it so far as to seize my sleeve outside the church and say, "I think it's lovely of you to pay this sort of *respect*, Inspector. You must see so many sad things."

Presumably seeing sad things would lessen one's respect.

I patted her hand and she seemed thoroughly satisfied. She was, or appeared to be, oblivious to the possibility that I was there to watch for a guilty move or suspicious strangers. I had gotten to the stage of thinking that one of them could have hired a killer. A killer who could creep into houses unseen and melt away afterward like smoke from a dying cigarette. Oh, well.

Altogether it was a very uncomfortable few minutes for everybody. Passim said something to Melanie that sounded musical and wasn't English, then explained it was a sort of wish for the soul, a custom of his country. She looked pleased. The rest stood around awkwardly, bound together by the fact that they hadn't the slightest idea how to cope, socially, with murder. Nobody mentioned the circumstances of the deceased's passing. Nobody until Alec became impatient with a situation that he viewed as hypocritical. In the middle of one of Mrs. Johns' loud sniffs, he turned to her and barked, "Well, *somebody* sure didn't like him."

While true, this put an end to the polite murmurs of sympathy.

Peter Erikson said, "Alec, we know that," in such a tone that the young man instantly shut up—a tone I had not heard Erikson use before. But the ice was broken. Mrs. Coyne turned to DeGraaf and, ignoring me, said, "I was wondering. What if somebody wore a single glove to hold the knife, and then just peeled it off and burned it in the fire?"

"I don't know," DeGraaf said. "I think it would have smeared the prints on the knife."

Maybe it was a mistake to let them know there had been prints on the knife, but we had to take theirs, and it seemed at the time it would make them more co-operative. All but one of them, at any rate. So I had hoped. I hadn't known at the time that for all the good it did I could have gone outside and taken the prints of everybody going by on the late bus.

I was about to point out that we had checked the ashes in the fireplace for buttons and remains of babrics or rubber, but why give things away free? Besides, the fire was really hot and I had no great confidence that there would be much left of anything but metal.

Passim excused himself from the interment on the grounds that he had surgical duty. Dr. Coyne wished Melanie, Mrs. Spruance, and Alec solace in their bereavement—wished it heartily and jovially —and, inviting his wife to meet him for lunch after she did some shopping, strolled away. The other doctors and the lawyer and nurses, seeing this trend toward breaking up, eagerly seized the chance. One by one they spoke with the family in good, solid, bedside tones, and escaped. That left us, the family, and the Johnses.

We trailed along to the cemetery in three cars. To my way of thinking my presence was an exercise in futility, but I am nothing if not thorough. Some-one other than these people had handled that knife. If one of these had been cold-blooded enough to hire a killer, he was hardly going to roll up his eyes and beg forgiveness just because he saw the coffin being lowered into the ground. One can always hope, of course, but relying on hope alone makes me grouchy.

DeGraaf seemed to be enjoying himself. The Johnses went in my car, the family car being crowded, and DeGraaf chatted the whole way with Mrs. Johns. It seemed she had a method for roasting chicken in a casserole that involved tarragon, white wine, and long cooking at low temperatures. When we got out of the car I hissed at him, "What do you think you learned by all that?"

"Something about chicken, Rob."

"Sure. But did you find out whether Mrs. Johns could or couldn't have killed Cotton? No, you didn't. Or have you forgotten why it is we're in a cemetery in the early morning feeling very uncom-fortable?"

"Look, Rob. Coming out in the car you were gnashing your teeth at the time it took to get here, right?"

"You bet."

"And about the time it was going to take for the interment and the time it will take to get back?"

"I certainly was."

"On the other hand, I found out something nice and useful, though not about murder. I passed the time pleasantly, and it didn't take me any longer to get here than it did you—did it?"

"You have no sense of what's appropriate."

"And while we're at it, you know perfectly well I do not see how Mrs. Johns could have anything to do with the murder."

"Oh, you don't? Why? Because she's willing to spend so much time and patience on chickens?"

"Not at all. As a matter of fact, this was a patient murder. It was planned for a long, long time. This isn't a bludgeon killing we've got here."

"Unless you're wrong. Unless it was totally impulse. Somebody saw the knife there, looked around and nobody was watching. Chance had put it in his lap. So he picks up the knife and strikes."

"Except that he had to come into the room unseen."

"Ahhh." I may have snarled at this point, for the minister, standing next to the grave, looked reprovingly in my direction.

The wind blew harder and I felt as cold as earth. Fortunately, this was not one of those affairs where they lower the coffin into the ground before your very eyes. Nor was there any symbolic dropping on of sod. I have always thought that was cruel to the relatives anyhow. The flowers were placed on the coffin, the minister said a prayer and a few other things, and then we all turned to leave, trusting, no doubt, to the people who ran the cemetery to do an honest job of the rest.

DeGraaf was watching Melanie and Peter Erikson with unusual intentness. I looked too. Erikson was standing near her, quietly, as he had through the whole thing. But they did not touch, except as we all started to walk slowly down the slope. For an instant she tripped over an unevenness in the ground and he caught her arm. Some understanding, or misunderstanding, passed between them and he dropped it again. They did not exchange glances.

Half a minute later, when Melanie had been looking behind herself for Mrs. Spruance, she nearly walked into Erikson, who had stopped just ahead. But she pulled herself up short, as if she did not want to touch him. It looked very much like an estrangement, and a funny time for it. She certainly didn't want to cry on his shoulder.

At the cars, she said, "We aren't having any refreshments at the house. There are no other relatives and—it just doesn't seem appropriate." Her voice caught.

"Certainly," DeGraaf said.

"And I'm going right back to work. Now. From here. Aunt Helen doesn't approve, but if we all just go on, people will stop talking sooner. I think."

"I'll drive you to work, Melanie," Erikson said.

"Could you drop Aunt Helen and Alec at home on the way?"

"Of course."

"Then the Johnses can take Daddy's car home. Or would it be better if they took Alec and Aunt Helen?" Her voice sounded very polite.

"Whatever you say, Melanie."

In the end, Erikson drove the family and the other cars went separate ways.

o　o　o

"Robert," DeGraaf said, as we swooped past the Chicago skyline on the Outer Drive, "what about the will?"

"What about it?"

"Is it going to be read, or what?"

"Yes. I think the lawyer is going to meet with them tomorrow night. But I talked with him already and he told me the provisions, if that's what you're driving at."

"It's what I'm driving at."

"He's told the family, too. Getting together is really only a formality. And naturally they may want to discuss things like keeping or selling the house and who invests the estate and so on."

"All right. But who gets the money?"

"Melanie, most of it."

"Is it a lot? I suppose it is."

"Sure. The man had been a practicing surgeon for more than thirty years. After his wife died he didn't go out much. He traveled some. Hunting trips. He'd go bag animals to stuff them. As he got older, though, he hunted less. Friends sent him animals to mount sometimes. Anyhow, he saved a lot of his money, and it appreciated."

"From the furniture I saw in that place, I'd say the household goods had appreciated, too."

"Okay. The estate altogether looks like it'll be worth nearly six hundred thousand."

"I see." He didn't sound pleased.

"What's the matter? Are you worried that Melanie might have killed her father for the money?"

"No, not really. She strikes me as less interested in money than most people."

"Always had a comfortable life. People like that

aren't hungry for cash."

"No, and anyway she'd get it eventually. I don't see her in a *hurry* for cash. She's not buying anything or going anywhere that I know of. The lawyer didn't make any sounds about old Cotton proposing to change his will, did he?"

"Nope. I thought of that. The will was made fourteen years ago and he hadn't said a word about it since. This lawyer does all Cotton's legal business, too. No, I don't think there's anything in that line of inquiry."

"And besides, that motive would apply to at least one other person."

"You mean Dr. Erikson?"

"Certainly. If he married Melanie, he'd have the money."

"They don't look quite on the verge of marriage now."

"No, but I think that's recent. They were warm to each other the night of the bridge game. Something has happened since."

"Maybe murder."

"It could be." DeGraaf rubbed his hands together. I couldn't tell whether it was his usual gesture of excitement or whether he was cold. "What did the will have to say about Alec and Mrs. Spruance?"

"Well, the house goes to Melanie, but she's supposed to give Mrs. Spruance a room there for as long as Melanie herself continues to own it."

"Rather a burden on Melanie if she should marry and her husband didn't want an old aunt around."

"I don't think Cotton cared about burdening people."

"No. What else."

"If Melanie sells the house, she is supposed to

rent Mrs. Spruance suitable lodgings' somewhere at her expense. I don't know about the legality of that provision, since Cotton didn't set aside any money to pay for it. The lawyer didn't sound too happy about that when he was telling me. However, I don't suppose Cotton would have been any more tactful about the lawyer's feelings than any of the rest of the world he came in contact with."

"Hardly. He would have considered the man another servant. That all for Aunt Helen?"

"No. She is to have fifty thousand outright 'in recognition of her relationship,' which is an odd way of putting it. But that ought to make her a bit more contented. It's little enough, though."

"And Melanie was to pay her rent."

"Yes. Actually, the interest Mrs. Spruance might raise on fifty thousand wouldn't generate nearly enough for rent plus living expenses these days. She might get four thousand a year from it, depending on how she invests it. So having Melanie get the bulk of the estate but pay Aunt Helen's rent as long as the old lady lives is not too unreasonable. That way Cotton's sister is provided for, but not given so much money that Cotton would feel much of his estate could later be willed away to somebody he didn't care for."

"Just the same, I'll bet Cotton put in the rent provision to show that his moral force was still strong even after his death."

"I agree, Gerritt."

"We're agreeing a lot all of a sudden. One of us must be making a wrong assumption somewhere."

"Sure."

"What about Alec?"

"Oh, I liked that part of it. Alec is left exactly

enough to finish college, and Cotton's line—he wrote it, not the lawyer, and the legal eagle's not too proud of this one, either—goes like this: 'so that Alec will realize, while he is in school, that what he accomplishes in the classroom is the fortune on which he must base his future life.' In other words, when he graduates he won't have a cent."

"Oho. I wonder whether he knows."

"He knows now. I told you the lawyer talked with the family. That was last night. What I don't know is whether he knew before Sunday night. The lawyer says *he* was never asked by Cotton to confide the terms to the family earlier. And not having been asked to by his client, he implies that thumbscrews would not have had it out of him. That's not to say Cotton couldn't have told them."

"I think that Cotton would have thought he exercised more dominance over them by keeping them guessing." DeGraaf looked down at my hands. I had them folded, but I was pumping the palms apart and together without being aware of it. I was more nervous than I thought I was. I had never before had a case like this; three days and I still couldn't give an honest guess on how it happened. DeGraaf did not mention my hands. He just said, "I don't know if it really matters whether Alec knew before the murder or not. A lot of people are killed for money, but a whole lot are killed for hate, too. In fact, I think there has to be a lot of hate in most killings."

"I do too, if you count generalized anger as hate. Alec surely feels that his uncle had been leaning on him for years."

"Of course, Alec could have gone off to work on a New Zealand sheep farm, and not depended on his uncle. Or courtesy uncle."

"Sure. But the fact that he'd been dependent on the man for years, Gerritt, was not going to make him fonder of Cotton. That's the trouble with charity."

# CHAPTER EIGHT

One thing DeGraaf was really useful for: getting me into the hospital without fuss, red tape, or introductions. I could have walked in as a policeman on a murder assignment, and been escorted just about anywhere. But what with introductions and other formalities, everybody is braced for your questions before you ask them. And as for walking in on my own and wandering around looking for somebody —forget it. They say that predatory fish in the sea choose for their victims those fish not swimming with the crowd, whose motions are uncoordinated, who, in a word, don't seem to know what they're doing. It's the same in hospitals. All the staff from the highest to the lowest march around purposefully, conveying a sense that they've been on the job at least thirty years. The patients go about in a sort of numbed trance, in little patterns, back and forth. But let an outsider come in and wander around looking for his destination and all the apparatus will descend on him, a foreign object, an item out of place, and possibly outside visiting hours as well. They'll get him and eject him.

Following DeGraaf you don't run that risk. He charges along, waving to half the staff and some of the patients, and you swim in his wake, being smiled at by people you've never met. They think you must be a hell of a fellow if you're his friend. All this without even carrying a stethoscope.

I had wanted to catch Erikson in his den, and apparently so did DeGraaf, an example of our temporary accord that showed my brain was softening. I ought to have been back in the office growling at people about tracing those fingerprints.

DeGraaf said, "Let's try to catch the Coynes, too. We should be able to get them on their way to lunch."

"What for?"

"I'd like to know what she meant by that remark about gloves."

"She'd been wondering how the thing was done. So have we all. So what?"

"Sure. Or maybe she meant she saw some gloves."

"She'd have said so."

"Oh? Come on. As a policeman, you know that isn't true. Besides, I get the impression that she plays her cards pretty close to the vest."

"You should know. She was your bridge partner, wasn't she?"

"Yes. I have an idea both Coynes have something on their minds. It makes them cautious in talking with us. I also think they may not feel very antagonistic toward whoever killed Cotton."

"That wouldn't make them unique."

All this time we were pounding down corridors

that looked absolutely identical. And the same people in them, too. Somewhere in the basement of this place they used discarded parts to turn out identical skinny little nurses in white caps with scrubbed faces and supercilious expressions. I was beginning to puff, and what really got to me was that DeGraaf wasn't even breathing hard. Anybody who says doctors don't get any exercise isn't looking in the right places.

After going through the same corridor about twelve times, we turned into one I hadn't seen before. It was out of Frankenstein by way of Busby Berkeley. Along the wall, separated only by those white curtains on chrome rods hospitals love so much, were rows of people hooked up by their veins to bubbling, gurgling machines. Well, all right, maybe not gurgling, but there was a lot of discreet humming coming from somewhere. The patients were reading magazines and napping and watching television, and in one case doing homework for school, just as if they didn't have a robot vampire attached to their veins.

Something grabbed my arm and I jumped. It was DeGraaf.

"Come on," he said. "They won't want you staring at them."

"Sure."

"I told you Erikson is a renal man. He also supervises the dialysis section."

"Oh."

"Will you come *on*, Rob?" He turned to an orderly. I assume it was an orderly. "Do you know where Dr. Erikson is?"

Getting a wave in the general direction of a white door, DeGraaf pushed it open and looked in. Dr. Erikson, wearing a white coat and carrying a tray of test tubes, turned around and saw us and jumped a foot. The tubes rattled. Now that's the kind of reaction I like.

"Peter?" said DeGraaf innocently. "Spare a minute?"

"Of course. Sit down."

This was vague, as there were only tables and one yellow oak swivel chair in the room, but DeGraaf perched on a table, so I figured they hadn't left any bubonic plague germs on the level surfaces and I did the same. Erikson, to be buddies, eschewed the chair also and perched on a facing table. He looked like a Broadway baritone sitting on a fiberboard fence, about to sing to the heroine. This guy was too handsome to survive.

"Are you and Melanie—or Dr. Cotton—on the outs?" I asked.

Erikson looked at me and took a breath, but he was too polite to tell me it was none of my business. "I hope not permanently," he said.

"I'm sure the whole thing has been very upsetting," DeGraaf butted in.

"It surely has. We're all sort of sickened, I guess."

"I think the Inspector is wondering whether there's any special reason that he might need to know . . ." DeGraaf let his voice trail off, not quite asking whether one of them saw the other commit murder and found it damping to romance.

"No, I don't think so," Erikson said slowly. He seemed actually to be considering it. "Melanie is kind of paralyzed, I think. It's a very good thing she's gone back to work. The more distance she puts between herself and the event, the better she'll feel."

"Dr. Erikson," I said, "don't you think it's time

to tell me why you tried to get into the library the morning after the murder?"

"But I told you."

"Making sure it was guarded? It's a good story for one thought up on the spot. But you could have made sure without going in."

"Well, I didn't *think* I could. I believed I had seen one of your men go in, so I hoped he was on duty there. But I wasn't sure and it could have been somebody else, couldn't it?"

"Maybe. Go on."

"That's about it. I looked in and didn't see anybody, but someone could have hidden behind a table or the bookcase. So I stepped inside. Then I noticed your man was there, in a shadow. That's why I hadn't seen him. I was relieved and I left."

"You didn't look relieved."

"I don't know what you mean. I wasn't *happy*. My prospective father-in-law had just been killed. My fiancée was distraught. But on the point about the room being guarded, I was relieved."

He did a good job, but I had interviewed lots of people and I was convinced he was lying.

"Now let's stop all this bickering," DeGraaf said. "Peter, would you explain to the inspector what you do here?" He waved his arm at the hall outside.

"Of course."

I thought Erikson would resent DeGraaf's abrupt change of subject, but he didn't. In fact he looked relieved and more than relieved. He looked delighted. I recognized the genuine look of the enthusiast invited to talk. He walked me to the door and faced me down the hall where the cubicles and machines were.

"Just a few years ago," he said, "everybody with

end-stage kidney failure eventually died. Everybody you see out there would have died months or years ago. Now we've got the kidney machine to clean their blood for them."

"Do they stay here?"

"No, they come in three days or so a week. How often depends on how serious their condition is and some other factors. In most cases, if they could get a transplant, a kidney from a living relative or a compatible donor who has just died, they wouldn't have to do this. But there aren't enough kidneys to go around. Especially with some rare tissue types, transplantation can be almost impossible. If more people would donate kidneys this wouldn't be necessary. Still, there's no doubt we're saving lives here."

"So everybody in Chicago who has kidney failure visits a place like this every week and gets overhauled?"

"No."

"No?"

"There aren't enough machines for everybody."

"So what do the others do?"

"They die."

"You just let them *die?*"

"*I* don't let them die. *You* let them die, in the sense that society permits it. If nobody living will donate a kidney, if the next-of-kin of accident victims won't make a kidney available, and if all our machines are in use and all the rest in the city are occupied, they die."

"Who decides who gets a machine?"

"It varies from city to city. There are committees. The committees are made up of doctors, clergymen, community leaders, that sort of person. And they just decide. Somebody has to. Mostly they try to favor the young, or somebody who has dependents. Generally they try to pick those who have the best medical prognosis, too. I've been on for a while. We try to switch around because it gets to be a strain. You can imagine how much fun it is to make decisions like that." He pushed his hands together hard and I looked away.

"I suppose money could buy more machines," I said.

"Machines, yes. The problem is, the cost of staffing and running a machine soon overtakes the initial cost of the equipment. Right now it costs thirty thousand dollars to care for one patient for one year. And it's going up. It's a very expensive business."

"What kind of patient do you turn down?"

"It depends on who's making the decisions. Very old people wouldn't get preference over a young person, other things being equal. Alcoholics are a bad risk; they don't take care of their health and sometimes they'll miss a dialysis and go into coma. Diabetics are bad risks. If we had two thirty-three year old males in good health and one had four children and the other had none, we'd pick the father. We'd have to." He looked at the tray of test tubes, and for a moment to him we weren't there. Then he glanced from the tubes to one of the cubicles in the hall. "We can tell from the blood, sometimes, if a person isn't taking care of himself properly," he said slowly. "With the number of people needing machines, we consider that to be an abuse of the program."

He looked back at the tubes. I shivered.

"Practically all of this could be eliminated if

dying people and families routinely donated kidneys," he said. "Oh, well. What did you want me to go into all this for, Gerritt? My job isn't going to help the Inspector in his job."

"I'm trying to educate him," DeGraaf said. "He needs a sort of rounding out."

As we were pounding back down the corridor, I asked, "Are you trying to show me a man could get used to making decisions about who should and who shouldn't live?"

"I don't know," he said.

We hit Coyne's office in the doctor's building next. The place was a slab structure next to the hospital. No windows on the first two floors and even the higher floors depended for light mostly on fluorescent lamps diffused by those things that look like ice cube trays. I've never understood why architects try to turn doctor's offices into approximations of operating rooms.

Coyne had tried to soften the appearance of his office by going in heavily for philodendrons, but the furniture was strictly contemporary waiting room. The secretary or nurse, probably a secretary dressed in white to look medical, had seen DeGraaf before, I guess, and she accepted me as somebody official without being told. Therefore we didn't get the bland consoling tones she had been using on the phone when we walked in. In fact, she tried to pump us. She had one of those reddish faces that looked peeled.

"What a shocking thing to have happen, Dr. De-Graaf, she said, priming the pump. "Right in front of Dr. Cotton's daughter." Pause. "Did you see it?"

"Unfortunately, I happened to be looking in the

other direction at the time," DeGraaf said. "Is Dr. Coyne in?"

Now, I had thought highly placed doctors would take fashionable one p.m. lunch hours, like bankers. But apparently their early surgical hours prepared them for early lunch.

"I'm awfully sorry," she said, looking pleased, "but he went out with Mrs. Coyne at eleven-thirty. I don't think they'll take long at lunch, though. He never does."

"I see."

"You know, it must have been more of a shock for Dr. Cotton's sister than anybody else. I mean, Melanie Cotton at least has medical training. And what a shocking time to have it happen! I mean after an evening of bridge. You might get robbed on the subway or stabbed in an alley, I mean—" She was fishing, and I wondered whether DeGraaf was going to give her anything.

"You'd hope not to be," he said.

"Naturally," she giggled. "Tell me, what did they *do?* Did they try to revive him? A whole roomful of doctors?"

"There was no question whatever of being able to save him."

"Ohhh." She savored this tidbit for a moment. "Ironic, isn't it? To have the evening end like that, after they sort of angled for an invitation."

DeGraaf and I, of course, did not glance at each other.

"Who angled?" he asked casually.

"Oh, Dr. Coyne. Cotton was over here a few weeks ago consulting about an artery graft and Dr. Coyne's wife had just won a bridge tournament, and Dr. Cotton politely complimented Dr. Coyne on it. And Dr. Coyne said, 'I'll bet that's why you never had us over to one of your bridge evenings. Afraid she'll beat you?' "

"What did Cotton say to that?"

"He said he never played, he just set up the hands. And Dr. Coyne said 'Oh,' and just let it hang for a few seconds and Dr. Cotton said, 'Well, you'll have to bring her to the next one. We'll see how good she is.' "

"She won."

"Oh! How nice! At least—"

"She won before the murder was discovered. That makes it all right."

She looked at him doubtfully, wondering whether he was making fun of her. "I didn't think you went on playing *after*," she said finally, and giggled at her quick wit.

"I think we won't wait for Dr. Coyne," said De-Graaf. "Thank you, though. We'll try to stop back." He gave her a big smile that seemed to go over very well.

"Whaddaya know," I crowed in the elevator. "That makes it very odd. That's news. I wouldn't have said Coyne liked Cotton at all."

"I don't think he did."

"And therefore, why wangle an invitation?"

"I have an idea why. We can ask later."

The pathology lab of the City Medical Examiner was in the basement of a three-story building in the same block as the hospital. It was separately funded by the city, but its closeness made it convenient: for people like DeGraaf, who consulted there, for hiring special equipment, for sending the hospital laboratories unusual samples that the medical examiner wanted help on, and so forth. Students of pathology assisted and trained in the ME's lab, as well as in the hospital labs. Altogether, there was a lot of interchange between the two centers.

Here we had white tiles all along the corridor and a concrete floor. It was the kind of building that makes your footsteps echo so that you think someone's following you. DeGraaf consulted a list on the bulletin board near a vacant desk.

"Dr. Melanie Cotton is in fourteen," he said.

We walked along, sounding like four people. Suddenly a door slammed open and a wild creature ran out. He was six feet tall and thin, with dark curly hair. His face was as white as the cold tile walls and he was using his knuckles to press in his lips. He sped past us and DeGraaf called cheerfully, "Bathroom's on your right!"

"Does this happen a lot?" I asked.

"Fairly. That was a student."

"Silly kid."

Now a head poked around the door the kid had run out of. It was Melanie Cotton herself, wearing a white lab coat with some unpleasant fresh stains. She saw us and her eyes opened wider, but she said only,

"How did he look? Is he all right?"

"Oh, sure. This his first day?"

"Very first."

We followed her into the room and I noticed she was wearing rubber gloves. They also had some smears on them. There was a sound of running water.

"I really should be going on with this," Melanie said. "I've got behind already, explaining things to the student. Can you talk while I work?"

DeGraaf said, "Sure."

The body lay on a table unlike an operating table. It was tilted toward the foot, for one thing, and unpadded steel, since of course, comfort for the patient was not a factor. It had an edge all the way around because of the water. The water came from a rod with holes in it, running across the top end of the table and looking very much like a lawn sprinkler aiming down. The water ran down around the body and into a drain at the lower end of the table.

Melanie trod on a floor pedal, said, "The liver is 1.4 kilograms, externally normal." Then she took the liver out of the scale and put it in a gravity-feed slicer with a rotating blade on the low end, very much like the one Morrie uses at the delicatessen I frequent. She stepped on another pedal to set the blade going.

Now, in the course of seventeen years on the force, I have seen everything. Fires, automobile accidents, suicides. And since I've been in homicide, every kind of shooting, stabbing, and poisoning the human mind can think of. Drowning victims several days old, where the skin looks larger than the body, corpses undiscovered for several days in the summer where the body begins to split the skin. But— I had had a long couple of days, and when I looked at the cadaver, pinned apart with retractors, open, without its liver, and somehow empty, my arms and legs started feeling cold. Then my head started to feel hollow. I looked up at the ceiling, rather than at the table, and the ceiling started buzzing. I heard DeGraaf call, "Down the hall and on your right!"

I swam very slowly out of there. Down the hall I found the bathroom, even though it was under water. After a few minutes I surfaced and I could see much better. I sat down on the counter next to a washbowl and was suddenly amazed to find myself looking into the face of a fellow human being with dark curly hair. He was sitting on the counter on the other side of the washbowl.

"She told me it would take another twenty minutes," he said with great precision, like a drunken man. "So if we stay here that long, we should be per-perfectly all right."

"Don't be scared," I said for some reason.

"No. I'll bet it happens all the time."

"Right. Um. Not to me it doesn't."

"What do you mean? Isn't this your first time?" His wits were clearing and he looked harder at me. I suppose he began to realize I was far too old to be a student.

"No. That is, I don't work here. I mean, I was just passing by with a friend." As if we'd just stopped in to take in a quick post mortem on the way to lunch. I'd be damned if I was going to admit to him that policemen get sick.

"Oh," he said.

We sat for some time, letting the physical and mental things get back into place. Finally, I said, "We'd better get back. They'll worry about us."

"Not me. I'm waiting another five minutes." He checked his watch to confirm his resolution.

"Well, I'm going. I'll tell them you're okay."

"What do you want to tell a lie like that for?" he asked. But I was heading out the door and just waved.

I had left the post mortem room door ajar, or to be more honest I had no closed it or even thought about it when I left. I started toward it, but then something about their voices stopped me. I poked my head cautiously in the small opening.

Melanie's head was on DeGraaf's chest, her arms

around his waist, though she was keeping the soiled gloves held away from him. He was patting her hair and she was crying. Being human, I backed up. Being a policeman, I stopped there.

"I never cry," Melanie said, sobbing and gulping.

"Why not?" DeGraaf asked.

"I'm not the type. At least I'm not supposed to be the type."

"Who says?"

"Oh, it's so stupid. I've always thought I was supposed to be firm and cool. You know. I'm sorry. Was I stepping on your foot?"

"Not at all. Here, let's peel those gloves. You can get another pair later."

"Umm. I'm sorry. It was just thinking about Daddy, I guess. I never really did please him, as far as I know. I was trying to be all the things at once that he'd have wanted. And now, of course, I never can."

"Are you crying again?"

"No, I'm not! Look at me! You're being silly. You're being very nice, too," she said, speaking more slowly. There was a moment of silence and I didn't know what to ascribe it to. I don't know what DeGraaf was up to in there, except that after a minute he said, "Now sit here and we'll talk. You've lost your assistant, anyway."

"Oh, oh." There was a scraping, like a chair being pushed. I assume Melanie jumped back up. "Do you think he's all right? He may have fainted and hit his head."

"No. They *either* faint or they go and be sick. Never both. Since he was walking when he went out, he is now sitting on the bathroom sink getting over it." The man no doubt had experience. I wondered why they didn't mention me.

"Everything is so strange," Melanie said. "Alec is acting funny. I think he wants to ask me for money and doesn't dare because he's always been so sullen with me. And Aunt Helen goes around perching on things as if she were just passing by, even though I keep telling her it's her home. I even told her I need her, and that's—"

The girl and DeGraaf started laughing. "That's absurd," DeGraaf finished for her.

"Yes," said Melanie. "Aunt Helen just spins her wheels. Still, seriously, she is someone to have in the house. She's a comfort. The house feels strange right now. I haven't got a superstitious bone in my body, but the place feels haunted."

"That's perfectly reasonable. When there's been a sudden death in a house, the people who live there tend to keep thinking they'll walk into a room and find the deceased in his usual chair. Every noise and creak sounds like him walking down the hall. It's just that the mind isn't used to having the patterns of a lifetime broken."

"In other words, you don't think I'm a nut."

"No."

"Aunt Helen twittering around is nice, somehow. And now that I don't know what's happening between Peter and me—everything is so difficult."

There was another silence. I was just thinking it was time for me to walk in when DeGraaf said, "What do you feel about Peter now?"

"I don't know. I haven't wanted to force the issue. Any decision. I'd like to wait a little while and see."

There was something she wasn't saying. Did she suspect Erikson of any involvement in the murder? DeGraaf must have wondered, too, for the next thing he said was:

"What sort of person is he?"

"Oh, very sincere. People often think he isn't because he's so good looking. But he is utterly unaware of the way he looks. He wouldn't think it was important, and he wouldn't understand why anyone else would pay attention to it. He's thinking about things that interest him—like expanding the dialysis program. He thinks now that they could partly automate it and cut the costs dramatically."

"I don't doubt that it'd help. Supervision must be a major part of the expense."

"Sure. And he has a list of twenty-seven points in the operation that could be handled by computer. He stays overtime to work on it. He's saying now that if they used the techniques available—I mean at the present stage of knowledge—they could handle two to three times as many patients."

"It would take money to set up."

"Naturally. Either a government grant, or maybe a grant from an individual to start it off—" Her voice trailed away. Was she thinking that Erikson would have considerable money if he married her? Maybe what he wanted was to streamline the dialysis program so that centers all over the country would take notice. Possibly the death of one difficult old man would be nothing compared to saving hundreds of thousands. I felt that Melanie had decided she had said too much.

DeGraaf didn't speak either. After a full two minutes I couldn't stand it any longer. I leaned around the doorjamb. Either he was kissing her or she was kissing him. I suppose it takes a little of each. Melanie's back was toward me and as luck would have it, DeGraaf stared right into my face.

Quickly I banged the door open all the way. Then

I walked in, stepping loudly, and paused suddenly. DeGraaf had stepped back from the girl and was looking at me quizzically. He wasn't annoyed, and he wasn't surprised.

"Robert. Come in," he said. "Did you find Melanie's student? So nice of you to go look for him."

I mumbled, "Shall I go get him?"

"He'll come back when he's ready."

"Anyway," Melanie said, and she giggled, "I've got another ten minutes or more. I've got a little delayed."

The phone rang. Melanie went to get it. It had a step-on button and funnel-shaped speaker, so that the pathologist did not have to touch it with soiled gloves, but the conversation could still be private. "Dr. Cotton," she said. In the white coat and general setting, I at last felt that the title looked right.

"Yes, he *is* here. Just a second." She pointed the phone at DeGraaf. "It's for you."

He raised his eyebrows and leaned his ear to the speaker. "Thanks. Hello? Gringo! How did you find me here? Oh. Okay. No, I like to see a man using his head. What's up?" We saw his face change, and Melanie, looking at him, knew something was really wrong. She bit her lip and waited.

"When, Gringo? Well, how serious is it? No, there's no reason for you to wait around; I'll just go right over. I appreciate your tracking me down. See you later." He hung up and looked at us for a second. At first I thought he was hesitating for effect, but immediately I realized he was angry.

"Mrs. Coyne—" he said "—fell or was pushed in front of a bus."

# CHAPTER NINE

Mrs. Coyne was neatly wrapped. I think the medical profession carefully wraps wounds after stitching them together not so much to keep out germs as to spare the patient's relatives the sight of the damage. What's under the white gauze, what they don't see, doesn't hurt them.

Thus Mrs. Coyne, with a white helmet of gauze wrapped around her head, looked neat and tidy. Just a little shaved scalp showed near one ear. There was a fresh white cast on her right forearm, with additional turns of gauze running down around her hand and up past the elbow. However, they had not tried to immobilize her arm. Possibly they did not think she was going to move. There were a couple of bruises on her face that they had not covered, only painted a brownish yellow. If it had not been for the tubes running into her and the machine that breathed for her, she would not have looked very alarming.

To DeGraaf's eye, however, this must have been

very grave looking indeed. There was a drawn look about his mouth. Dr. Coyne stood immobile in one corner. A large man in green surgical garb stood nearer the bed, and DeGraaf asked him a dozen questions about vital signs while I stared at Mrs. Coyne. I hardly knew her, but I thought she was not the sort of person to blunder in front of a bus while watching a thrilling flight of starlings overhead.

Also, I was no doctor, but I knew that when they had a machine do your breathing for you, you were not in good shape. Nobody seemed willing to say that she was dying. But I was going to treat this as a murder investigation right from the start, and not a fraction less seriously than that.

DeGraaf came away from his conversation looking ill.

"I should have made her talk," he said.

"Oh, come on!" I said. What could I tell him? After all, I was the person actually responsible for the investigation and I had not gotten to her in time, any more than he had.

"It happened over an hour ago," DeGraaf said. "They've had her through X-ray and the casting room in record time. The husband being a doctor makes a difference, I guess." He kept his voice down, but as far as I could see Coyne was not a hearing, thinking man. He looked as patient as a cigar store Indian.

"What's her condition?" I asked.

"They're trying to decide whether to try surgery." As he spoke, I saw the man in green pat Coyne on the arm and leave. Coyne also showed the responses of a wooden Indian. "The problem is," DeGraaf went on, "there's a seepage of blood behind the impact area that's putting pressure on the brain. My guess is that they'll decide to operate. I would."

"Why are they hesitating?"

"It's hazardous. She could die during surgery. Or later. Or she might not die at all, and just lie in a coma for years. Damn it to hell."

"I still say you couldn't have known."

"We all heard her ask about gloves. She could have simply had an idea. But it turns out she had a *glimpse.*"

He stood there, hating himself, and I couldn't think of anything to say that would cheer him up, so I just let him go at it. Maybe he would think of something. Maybe I would.

Dr. Coyne went on standing, just a few feet from his wife's bed, not moving. He had not turned nor appeared to listen while DeGraaf talked with the other man about Mrs. Coyne's condition. I guess he'd been through all the same questions himself and nothing could worry him more than he already was.

So we all stood there in silence and stared at the mummy in the bed.

What finally broke the spell was the door opening and Melanie Cotton entering the room, out of breath and very pale. "I had to finish—" she said, and stopped and looked. We had left her with the post mortem, of course, but she had been distressed then at the news. I wondered how well she had finished her job before coming here. It hadn't taken her long.

And now that made four of us looking at Mrs. Coyne. Melanie took in the significance of the machines and tubes with a doctor's eye. She started to say, "Is it as bad as it looks?" then belatedly recognized Dr. Coyne. She went to him. Touching his arm, she said, "What a terrible thing! Can you go somewhere and sit down?" She pressed his arm to get his attention.

He turned to look at her, which was the first move he had made, as far as I could see. She steered him toward the door with her hand on his arm and he went along obediently, as if he had just been waiting for someone to take charge. We went along too. There was nothing we could do for Mrs. Coyne. The nurse in the glass booth who kept watch on the intensive care unit did not look up as we left.

Melanie got Coyne into one of those small rooms with steel cabinets, swivel chairs and tables, the sort of room that should have a sign on the door reading "Miscellaneous," and we all sat. I found a phone in the corner. Since the others were taking a while to absorb what had happened, I grabbed the phone, got the switchboard, and had them put me through to headquarters. Fortunately, Peter Wharten was in my office.

"Peter, I'm at Hastings Hospital. Have you heard about an accident in front of the hospital about twelve-thirty or a little later? Well, it was one of the Cotton murder witnesses. Good. I'm amazed and delighted to think that somebody is on the ball." I stopped a second and considered. With Coyne sitting right here, I didn't want to come out and say that I wanted to treat this as attempted murder. On the other hand, that was exactly what I intended to do. Of course, that was one reason it was fortunate Peter was on deck. He could read between the lines.

"Can't talk freely?" he said, into my silence.

"Right. We're lucky that Mrs. Coyne wasn't killed, but we're going to handle it as seriously as if she were—"

"You think somebody meant murder?"

"Right. Get to the patrolmen who were first at the scene and have them amplify their reports. I mean every detail they can remember. Who they saw where, what the bus driver said—and by the way, have them come in later so that I can talk with them. Find out whether anything was dropped at the scene by anybody. Who called the emergency service? If anybody got the names of witnesses, find out who. Bundle copies over to me here. I'll leave word where I'll be at the desk. Then I want two boys to go and comb the scene. Don't send that idiot Cramer. Get Ted and maybe Elwin. Tell them to fingerprint the light posts and stop signs if they have to, but to cover everything. If I find out later there was important stuff on the scene we overlooked, somebody is going back to crosswalk patrol. Now when they get done, have them come and tell me about it. Okay?" Okay, of course, doesn't mean is it okay with him; it means it's okay with me if he starts doing what I say immediately.

I hung up and swivelled. Our little group was still looking catatonic, except that Melanie had thrust a can of juice from one of the cabinets into Coyne's hand. "The next thing," I said to the room at large, "is to find out where everybody was. That should be easy with most of them, since it's a working day. They were probably in full view of somebody."

DeGraaf groaned. Coyne looked up, but with no understanding in his face.

"Poor Rob," DeGraaf said. "You don't know hospitals. The thing must have happened at quarter of one. That's just the end of the lunch hour."

"So? Was it quarter of one?" I asked Coyne.

"What? Um, yes. I guess so. They called me about—about five of."

"All right. Let me start by asking where you and Dr. Cotton here were at the time. No offense."

"Where I was?" Coyne said, like a man who was thinking about something else. "Glynis and I came back from lunch. She came up to the office with me, but she left about twenty of one, I guess. I hung up my coat and started going through a stack of records. I'd just started when they called. That was all."

"You didn't go out of the office?"

"No. Yes. I went out to the bathroom in the hall."

"Was your secretary in the office, so she'd know where you were and how long you were gone?"

This was really getting down to it. I thought any minute he'd start resenting the questions, since they so clearly implied a suspicion of him, but he hardly appeared to notice that he and I were talking.

"My secretary? She isn't really due back in the office until one. She got in a little early. She always does. I don't know when, but soon after I got in."

"And she didn't go out again?"

"Yes, she went right out to get water for her coffee pot. The ladies room is farther along the corridor."

"Oh." Unless the secretary had been staring at her watch incessantly, we were in trouble over this one.

"And you see," said DeGraaf, making the problem clearer, "the bus stop is about thirty seconds' walk from the main desk, and not more than two minutes' walk away from any part of the hospital, if you know the shortest route. And you would, if you worked here."

I sighed. "What about you, Melanie? Dr. Cotton?"

"I really would rather you called me Melanie," she said. "At quarter of one I was just back from lunch and in the P.M. lab. However, the only person there was deceased. The student got there around five of one. He was early at that, being new, I guess. He's supposed to be there at one o'clock."

"Do you mean to tell me, Gerritt—" and I may have shouted a little "—that in a hospital where everybody does everything right on schedule, with a full team of students and nurses and orderlies hanging around, that nobody is going to know where anybody was?"

"Robert, you have to realize that it was half past lunch and a quarter of work."

"Jeez."

"Also, in a hospital, everybody on the job is doing something. They're moving around. It's not the kind of environment where people are all sitting at rows of desks in sight of each other. The only place people would be together and certain of it for a long period of time would be in surgery. And most operations would be over by now."

The glorious vision I had entertained of cutting the suspect list at least in half was evaporating. And I didn't realize in my annoyance that I was being inconsistent. To begin with, it was perfectly evident from the fingerprints that none of the so-called 'witnesses' at the bridge party had actually stabbed Cotton, so what was I fussing about? The same stranger whose face we had not yet seen simply walked up to Glynis Coyne at the bus stop and gave her a push. Maybe. Secondly, I was behaving as if I were certain she had been pushed, and pushed intentionally. While in my opinion she was no daydreamer, there must have been a terrific crowd there at noon; there always was. And everybody wanted to get a seat on the bus. She might have fallen or the crowd in general could have surged forward, making her lose her balance on the curb. If someone in the crowd had shoved too hard, trying to get a place in the front, he surely was not going to rush up to us and admit it. The whole crowd would just fade away into the population and no one would ever be the wiser.

DeGraaf was looking at me. He may have been thinking too that it was odd of me to be so hot on the trail of the bridge party, for he said, "Of course, you have to follow up everything. Would you like me to have the rest of them sent up here? I can have the person at the desk page them."

It was done. I saw Dr. Passim, who at twenty of one had just left the cafeteria where he had eaten egg salad sandwiches with two friends who could vouch for him, and had started toward the ward where the nurse could vouch for him. He was certain that not enough time had elapsed for him to go out to the street and come back. That was nonsense. He could easily have seen Mrs. Coyne crossing the lobby and followed her. He was hopeful his friends and the nurses would remember to the minute when he was with them. I knew too much about people to agree.

When Peter Erikson came in to see us, he smiled wanly at Melanie. But he did not take her hand, perhaps because she simply smiled and then looked away. As for the time Mrs. Coyne was injured, he had much the same problem as everybody else; he claimed that he had never left his wing, or indeed his ward.

"I brought my lunch with me again today, so I just stayed around to keep an eye on the machines. I never left at all." Two nurses, consulted by phone, confirmed that they had not seen him leave, and had the impression that he had been there continuously. But there were two back stairs in the section. Also, they had been serving lunch to the dialysis patients at the time and were very busy. It was absurd, they said, to imagine they could stare at Dr. Erikson the whole time.

He left and I phoned the Johnses. Mrs. Johns said she and her husband had been cleaning all morning since returning home from the funeral. They had been more or less in each other's sight since. Of course, they could make that claim, whether it was true or not. She also told me that Alec Spruance had not come back to the house after the funeral that morning and that his aunt had returned but gone out around noon. Aunt Helen had said she was going to church.

I phoned Pryczyk but neither he nor his wife was home. It all began to seem pretty hopeless. I knew what I had to do. I had to find some record of that set of fingerprints, even if it meant sending to every state individually and then starting on Canada and Mexico.

"The fact is," I said to DeGraaf, "we've known an outsider did it, right from the beginning. And either he pushed Mrs. Coyne or she simply fell and it's a coincidence. Somebody who heard her question at the funeral could have called the man and told him to lie in wait for Mrs. Coyne. Whichever, I'm going back to the office to get to work. I'll leave word at the desk for the men to report there."

DeGraaf didn't answer, Coyne was looking at his shoes, and Melanie Cotton appeared to think I wasn't speaking to her, as in fact I wasn't. We had another profitless silence.

Finally, DeGraaf unfolded his arms.

"I've had enough of this," he said, just as if the whole thing was up to him. "You can go back to your office, and I hope you turn up some useful facts. But basically, you're on the wrong track. We've got to look closer into Cotton himself and the people who were there that night. It's my fault this happened. I've been meandering around asking polite questions and look what we got for it."

"You're jumping to conclusions," I said. He went on as if I hadn't spoken.

"So now I'm going into detail on everybody, whether they like it or not."

"And so am I," said Melanie.

We both stared at her. She stood there, slim but somehow solid and determined, clenching her hands. As we looked, she added, "Well, I've had enough of this, too. And it was *my* father who was killed. And now Glynis Coyne! If we don't clear this up, who knows what will happen next; and the whole lot of us will be under suspicion for the rest of our lives!"

This discussion, of course, did not say much for their faith in me and the police department. But they were upset and I let it go.

"They weren't expecting me back to work so soon, anyway," she said. "Henry can do it for a while. He's always there anyhow. And I," she said to DeGraaf, "am coming with you."

"Good," he said.

Coyne was still sitting. Melanie added, "Except first I'm going to take Dr. Coyne back to his office to rest. And I'd better have him sent up a sandwich and coffee. I imagine he'll be here until—for quite a while."

o    o    o

I went to my office to be among people I could yell at. DeGraaf and Melanie went to Dr. Cotton's office. Not to Melanie Cotton's, but to the office in the Hastings Medical Building that Adam Cotton had used.

When DeGraaf explained later what they had checked into, it was clear they had not kept anything from me, though I half suspected that at the time. In fact, they came running to me the next morning with what they had found, rather like retrievers.

I can well imagine Melanie, with her tendency to force herself to face up to things squarely, standing on the threshold of her father's office. It was the first time she had been there since his death. The secretary was gone, and rumor was that she had not attended the funeral because she had been about to quit in any case and thought it would be dishonest to pretend grief. Cotton, no doubt, had upbraided her once too often. Wonderful fellow, Cotton. The secretary, by the way, was playing bingo at church during the fateful bridge game.

DeGraaf said, "I want to go through your father's files. All of them. All the way back." He didn't give Melanie time to indulge in nostalgia in the doorway. "How far back do they go?"

"As long as he's been practicing. I'm certain of that. I don't think he even removed deceased patients from his files. He said you never knew when insurance companies or the government might want something. And then, he also kept all his data because he might need it for an article."

"I suppose as long as there was space enough it would be less trouble to keep them than cull them. If Robert ever puts a name to those fingerprints, we'll have to go back through the files for that name. Right now, though, we want any file on any person connected with your father's death. Guests and employees and relatives."

It was three in the afternoon when they started. The job would have been completed more quickly if all the cases had been alphabetized in one long series. However, DeGraaf soon found that Cotton had started new files three times in his career, and in addition maintained a holding file for patients who had been treated in recent years but had no special reason to come back. There was one file covering patients he had treated while a medical student and intern in Boston. There was a second file from a hospital in New York City where he had done his residency. The third, and by far the largest, was the file of cases he had treated since coming to Hastings Hospital, but which were non-current. Then there was a small cabinet full of folders on active cases.

Melanie and DeGraaf made a list of the names they were looking for: Coyne, Glynis; Coyne, Liam; Erikson, Peter; Johns, John; Johns, Mary Ellen; Passim, Ibid; Pryczyk, Bart; Spruance, Alec; Spruance, Helen; Spruance, Leonard (long deceased, Helen's husband). Melanie made no objection to the inclusion of Peter Erikson.

"What do you suppose Mrs. Pryczyk's maiden name was?" DeGraaf asked, not expecting an answer.

Melanie said, "Well, we should have Mrs. Coyne's, too, if we want to be complete. And we ought to look up Aunt Helen under Cotton, Helen, also. But really, if he had had a family member as a patient, I think I would have heard about it. It isn't usually done."

"We'd better include your mother, too."

"Why? I know he wouldn't have treated anyone *that* close to him. Not for anything serious."

"He might have a record, even if he had sent her to somebody else. It would be interesting, wouldn't it, if Dr. Coyne had once had your mother as a patient and bungled it?"

"Oh, lord," said Melanie. But she added, "Her name was Claire Ellison Cotton."

"Well, pick a file for yourself and we'll start."

"Which one do you want?"

"Oh, whatever you don't," said DeGraaf.

"No, you first," said Melanie and then she started to laugh. DeGraaf laughed too. "This is ridiculous," she said, still smiling. "I'll take the New York one and I bet I beat you."

"We'll see about that."

But it was slow going for both of them. The files themselves were both typewritten and handwritten, but all of the labels were handwritten, in so many hands, good and bad, that it was obvious that Cotton had changed secretaries very often all his working life. DeGraaf unearthed a form with Melanie's mother's name on it, but it told only of sending her to X-ray for a broken finger. The orthopedic man must have taken over after that. Under cause of accident was the notation, "playing croquet."

Melanie smiled at that. "I didn't even know they used to play croquet," she said. "I wish I remembered more about her."

Suddenly DeGraaf jumped up.

"What did you find?" asked Melanie, alarmed.

"Nothing. I just remembered something important I meant to do. My brain has had a shock, I suppose. Does this phone still work?"

"I don't see why not. I never asked to have it disconnected."

It worked. But DeGraaf's fingers fumbled he was in such a hurry. After a wrong number, he got Dr. Coyne in his office.

"Liam? Gerritt DeGraaf. Sorry to bother you. How is Mrs. Coyne? Oh. I think that's good; you would have had to come to surgery sooner or later. What about the EEG? Well. It could be worse. Listen, I wouldn't bother you if this weren't important. When you and Mrs. Coyne had lunch this noon, did she say anything about the murder? No, I mean anything specific. Did she say anything about a glove? Well, about anybody having a glove or removing a glove? I see. No, I heard her say that, too. It may not; I didn't think it was important at the time. One other thing. Would you ask to have either a guard or a nurse posted by her bed when she comes out of surgery? I don't know, but it could be. Well, I just don't think the nurse in the booth is enough, even though she can see her. Thanks, Liam. Chin up. Calgary's the best. He'll bring her through."

Melanie looked at him as he hung up.

"She's still in a coma," DeGraaf said. "Slow pulse, subnormal temperature. They've been discussing the angiogram back and forth and they've decided to go in and try to relieve the pressure."

"What about the EEG?"

"He didn't quite say. I don't think it's flat, but they're worried."

"I should think they would be. It's ironic, in a sad way."

"What is?"

"Dad was always in favor of pulling the plug on a brain damaged patient who couldn't recover. I was always against it. Coyne was one of the people on the staff who strongly agreed with Dad. I said we didn't know enough; we didn't know for certain when it was hopeless. Dad said if you had a flat EEG, brain death was certain and you ought to turn the equipment over to somebody who might benefit from it."

"And now Coyne, you think, may be confronted with exactly that problem?"

"I hope he won't, but it certainly looks possible."

"You think he'll act differently with someone he loves?"

"I think Liam is a lot more emotional than he looks."

"A lot of relatives ask to have the family member be allowed to die without interference."

"Yes it's not a case of putting people out of their suffering if they're not conscious. Maybe I'm unnecessarily fearful, but it seems to me the only consistent position, the only one you can apply in all cases across the board, is to require physicians to try to maintain life as long as possible."

"It's an easier position. It's simpler. But the fact that you have to make hard decisions if you're willing to consider cutting off a hopeless patient doesn't make the decision wrong."

"I'm not sure it's the hard decisions I mind, Gerritt. It's drift. I'm concerned that over time the decisions might become easier and easier. It might be done more often and with less reason."

They went back to the files. Melanie got through the New York series and then went back through the Boston drawers without turning up any familiar names. DeGraaf did the current patients without finding anything important. He turned to the Chicago inactives.

It began to darken outside and Melanie flicked on the second bank of overhead fluorescent lights. She sighed and kept on through the Boston records. DeGraaf's swivel chair creaked loudly in the late afternoon silence.

Then he said, "Oh-oh."

"What?" said Melanie, sitting up as if a strange hand had touched the back of her neck.

"Sorry. I didn't mean to startle you. Look at this." He held out a manila folder.

She took it, trembling a little, her eyes wide. This was too much strain for her, DeGraaf thought, as he realized too she would never admit the fact.

She looked up from the folder after not more than thirty seconds.

"Baby girl Johns?" she asked. "And the parents were John and Mary Ellen Johns."

"Right."

"1942. That was before Daddy hired them. It was before I was born."

"Read the rest."

"Ventricular septal defect. That's—oh, right. That's a congenital heart defect where the lungs get a better supply of blood than the rest of the body?"

"Yes. They would probably have tried to go in and band the pulmonary artery to force more blood to the rest of the body. That would only delay things. If it's successful, then you have to go back in and repair the hole in the heart when the child is older."

"But it wasn't successful. She died. The baby died."

"During surgery," said DeGraaf.

"Are you saying they blamed Dad?"

"How do I know? The baby was only a few days old. It must have been a severe case or they would have waited a little while. So the baby may have looked very ill, even to the parents. Blue extremities and so on. Surgery on infants was far less safe those days. They may have expected the child to die and may have been grateful to your father for doing what he could."

"As he did. He must have."

"Yes, I think he always did."

"You know, Gerritt, I've been thinking while I was looking through these files, and reading one or two here and there—some of the things he did years and years ago, artery repairs long before we had silastic and hypothermia and so on. The cures he achieved. He was—really fine."

"At his job, as Coyne said, he was the best there was." He took the file from her. "I understand what you mean, though. So many people are unnmoved by his death."

"It doesn't seem fair."

"I know. They found him hard to get along with. And he wasn't very tolerant of more fallible people. You knew that. People don't miss him the way they might miss somebody who was warmer and friendlier and maybe made more mistakes. It isn't fair, because in losing him there's a real talent and decades of experience lost."

"I'm glad Dr. Coyne said that." She paused, looking lonely. "No, I'm all right. I'm just getting used to the change. What about the Johnses? You can't possibly believe they moved into this house and then dug themselves in and waited twenty-four years to kill Dad. It sounds silly. And besides silliness, they're just not like that."

"I believe that. But we have to let Rob know. It wouldn't be right to hide it. The Johnses must have intentionally decided to leave it out when Rob and I spoke with them."

"He'll jump to conclusions and hound them with questions. He's going to be after them day after day. He'll keep coming back—"

"They're pretty solid people, Melanie. They can take it. But I don't think he will do it that way. He'll ask them about it, but without any evidence at all that they're involved, he'll just have to let it drop."

"Even if you're right, even that—stirring up old pain. Their daughter would have been in her thirties now. They could have had grandchildren."

"Melanie, you've got to stop thinking like this. You're not personally responsible for everybody."

"I thought they had never had any children and maybe never wanted any. They seemed so well suited as a couple."

"Maybe they had to be. Not only because they lost the child but because their job calls for them to work together as a team."

"Why didn't I ever wonder before about whether they were happy? They were such a part of things. Are they happy, do you think?"

"I'm sure of it. They have the gift of being happy where they are. Very few people seem to achieve it."

"I think you have it, Gerritt."

"Sometimes."

The house on Schiller Park was silent and most of the windows dark when they arrived. Melanie let herself in with her key, not ringing for Johns. But the alert old butler heard the sound of the door closing in the front hall and came up to greet them.

"Will you have some coffee or sandwiches, Miss Melanie?" he asked. His face was smooth and kindly; he was glad to see her home. She nodded, swallowing once. DeGraaf could feel her thinking that this man did not kill Adam Cotton. Indeed he sensed in her an impulse to look over at him as if to say, "See what sort of man this is," but she resisted it. After a second or two she must have felt her nod to be ambiguous, for she added with a smile, "Coffee and sandwiches both, if you would. We skipped dinner."

Johns left, pleased, walking straight and unhurried to the kitchen.

"Do you mind if I wander around?" DeGraaf said. "I should have warned you before we got here that I'm hoping I'll get a feeling about your father. It's not easy to say, but except for some of the random violence cases, murder has as much to do with the character of the victim as the character of the killer."

"You make it sound as if he asked for it," she said, shivering.

"No, I don't mean that. I think there are some murder victims who are more similar to suicides than anything else. Young desperate males who keep getting into fights might be one sort. But all I mean in this case is that there are reasons why someone is killed. The event doesn't happen out of nowhere. There's as much leading up to it as there are consequences after it. I'd like to just nose around and see what your father was like."

"From the house? Certainly, go ahead." She

stood gamely waiting, like a puppy, willing to follow its master anywhere.

DeGraaf went down the hall to the library. The stuffed and mounted animals went through a variety of expressions as he passed, changing as his angle of view changed. He came to the oak door. When he shoved it, it squeaked. Inside the library a policeman he had never met looked up from Cotton's wing chair.

"This room is off limits," he said.

"My name is Gerritt DeGraaf. If I could ring up Inspector Craddock for you—"

"Oh. No, don't bother. You're on the list. He said to let you in if you came. Funny, though. He said you were a tall, skinny, nosy-looking guy." Melanie giggled in the background. "Nobody from the house goes in, though."

"Not even Dr. Cotton? If we watch her every minute?"

Melanie said, "Don't bother about it. I'll get the sandwiches and meet you later in Dad's study." She looked at the policeman. "Would you like a plate of sandwiches and coffee?"

"No, thanks, ma'am. I just had some. The butler brought them an hour ago." The policeman was young and pale-skinned, and very impressed at being waited upon by a butler.

"Good for Johns," Melanie said. She went out, closing the creaking door.

DeGraaf, as he looked around, asked, "Anything happen during the day?"

"The kid wanted to get in. I guess that's all."

"Alec Spruance?"

"Yeah," said the policeman with a mouth of distaste. Alec was not making friends.

"Mmm."

DeGraaf at first simply circled the room, hoping that a new idea might strike him, either from his subconscious or from observation of the room itself. The windows? No, it was absolutely impossible that anyone had climbed in either window during the game. It was impossible to the point of being absurd to waste time on it. Secret passages or hidden panels in the room? The police technician had checked for that. But in addition DeGraaf was certain of two things: this house was built with a degree of solidity and architectural honesty that was inconsistent with secret passages, and second, any man appearing from a secret panel would have been far more noticeable than any similar man simply walking in the door.

Down the chimney? That was even sillier. It was too narrow; he looked up to be certain. Moreover, there had been a blazing fire. And thirdly, the same objection applied as in the case of secret panels. Had anyone stepped out of the fireplace, one of the card players or dummies would be sure to notice. This was a murder that depended heavily on looking ordinary, on being not worth noticing.

Could someone have hidden under the big wing chair? Surely, even if it were possible, he could not have left the room afterward. The same problems applied to leaving as entering, and there had been a guard in the room continuously since the murder.

The policeman had walked over to the windows and DeGraaf tipped the big chair over. It was skirted to the floor, so the underside wasn't visible when it was upright. However, its legs were only seven inches long and above them was a solidly padded bottom. No one could have squeezed under it, much less have crawled out and then back under again.

DeGraaf's eye fell on the manuscript of Cotton's article, still lying on the table in front of the fireplace. He sat down in Cotton's chair and started to scan it. What an odd document it was, in a way—all hard sentences, short and clipped, never a statement of uncertainty, never a "maybe", not even the faithful old "it could be argued" to mute the tone. Adam Cotton simply stated his case, presented his facts and examples, and assumed any intelligent man would agree. Given the subject matter, what he called the necessity of letting hopeless cases die, most men would have included at least some statement of regret or some hope that in a better day, with more equipment and better skills, such decisions would not be necessary. Not Adam Cotton. He made no attempt to make his view palatable to the reader.

DeGraaf laid it on his knee, thinking that he had gone a little farther into Cotton's mind. Another idea struck him. He paged back through the whole thing to check whether any pages were missing. But the numbers were consecutive and the sense flowed from page to page.

Then abruptly a memory returned. There was an aspect of the manuscript he had not focused on before. Cotton, on the night of the card party, had remarked that he would tell in his paper how two people died. DeGraaf quickly flipped over the pages. Yes—there it was. Jimmy Wigoda and Eileen Lee. Cotton had named them at the time. But what words had he used? Something like "implications of their deaths." DeGraaf read through the passages. Cotton used the two cases as examples of people, hopelessly injured, brains destroyed insofar as the EEG could show, who had required months of equipment and personnel to keep them alive. And then they had, quite naturally, died.

But what if someone at the bridge party believed that by "implication" Cotton had meant something about the manner in which they had originally been injured? Or, more likely, the way in which their cases were handled at the hospital? They were clearly cases Cotton knew first-hand; therefore, they must have been treated at Hastings. The chance that one or more people present the night of Cotton's death had also been involved in the cases was fairly good. What if somebody had made an error? What if someone were guilty of criminal mismanagement?

DeGraaf decided to get to the hospital computer and pull records on both patients as soon as he could.

DeGraaf stood and stuck his toe in the ashes of the fire. There were no pages missing as far as he could tell. Did his idea about the two patients suggest that Cotton was taunting one of the guests that night? Was he torturing someone, not even intending to give any details about Wigoda's or Lee's treatment in the paper? And did that imply that the murder was one of impulse, after all? How could it be?

There were few of the ashes left. The police had been through them and had found no cloth, zippers, or buttons, and no large sheets of burned paper.

Certainly the manuscript was as Cotton had left it when he died.

He stared into the dead fire, seeing it alive as it had been on Sunday night. Methodically, he tried to become Cotton himself, in this dark house, surrounded by the dead animals he had mounted and the family he had shown no sign of loving. And a hot fire that was not bright enough to light the corners of the room.

DeGraaf walked out of the library, preoccupied. He found Melanie in the study with food and drink and smiled at her automatically, still trying to feel Adam Cotton. Sensibly, Melanie did not interrupt him. She passed sandwiches and poured coffee. DeGraaf did not sit down to eat, but prowled, studying the room. Most of the books on these shelves were medical texts or bound volumes of journals. There was a smattering of books in Latin, and a few, such as *Upland Game Shooting* and *Great Guns* which were hunting books. No fiction.

There were no family photographs whatever, no image, portrait, or sculpture of Melanie's mother. Or Melanie either.

On one wall was a large Audubon painting of two ruffed grouse on the wing. It looked like an original and DeGraaf did not doubt that Cotton could afford it. On the wall behind the desk was a small Lynn Bogue Hunt of mallard ducks. A tiger in black on white on the third wall carried a signature in Chinese characters. The paper looked old. Other than these, the room held only two dark green leather chairs, the old oak desk, oak bookcases, and an Afshari rug. The window was covered with louvered shutters, darkly stained.

As he told me later, DeGraaf continued to try to think himself into Cotton's life. For a few moments he worried that his withdrawal was rude to Melanie, but he had in the back of his mind her own stated need to find out, so he excused himself. He thought of a man who had liked these dark, traditional rooms, who liked things done properly, and who cared, or thought he cared, for nothing but accuracy. A man with a bright mental focus on what interested him and dark edges to his mind. Slowly, thinking of Cotton, DeGraaf became aware of a vague, dark dread, as if a type of life force that Cotton had not known existed was hovering malignantly over the old man. DeGraaf was frightened. He moved uneasily. Cotton had been stalked by something that had grown out of his own personality and had finally turned and destroyed him.

DeGraaf's legs would not let him stay in the study. He strode out the door and into the hall with the heads. A tiger, an antelope and a cougar were frozen on the walls, all methodically mounted, perfect in detail, all very dead. On a table a snowy owl clutched a pine branch.

Just barely conscious of Melanie trotting alongside, DeGraaf loped through the hall, past the parlor with the pronghorn, and into the back regions of the house. Into the kitchen he went, and there must have been an odd look on his face, for the Johnses stepped back and said nothing. He opened a door, but behind it was only a pantry full of canned goods and bottles. He looked around the corner behind an antique ice door and found the stair leading down.

The cellars were dark and the ceilings low, as in most very old houses. He lighted the bare bulbs hanging from old black cords, but the place remained mostly in shadow. DeGraaf poked his head into the first room he saw, partitioned off from the cellar with pine boards so old that they were a deep golden orange. It was a root cellar, with stacks of ancient greenish glass canning jars dusty on the shelves. Beyond that door was an alcove with firewood, bone dry and grayish with dust. Spiders had been weaving the logs together for years. In the distance was a hulking coal furnace under a dense cocoon of plaster. Opposite the furnace another door led away, squeezed under support beams.

DeGraaf walked into the room and pulled the string to the overhead light. He found it to be a fluorescent. It was the only fixture in the basement that gave adequate light.

This was Adam Cotton's taxidermy workroom. There were glass jars of chemicals, books on taxidermy, and rows of scalpels on a leather-backed rack. Along one wall were a few animal skulls. A spraying stand held a walleye pike, finished and painted but not varnished. A bag of plaster was on a high shelf against the wall nearest the furnace, away from sources of dampness. A jeroboam labelled "alum-salt-borax tawing liquor" stood on the concrete floor. Two large cans of borax, one so light as to be nearly empty, the other full, were on the table. Even the used can was clean. There was nothing spilled or out of place anywhere. It was just as DeGraaf's idea of Cotton would have led him to predict. And he guessed that in here, unlike the rest of the house, Cotton did his own cleaning up.

In a wax dissection dish, a bird skin with some bones attached was pinned down. There was an oilcloth over it, but the bird had dried. Perhaps Cotton had been removing the flesh of the bird prior to filling the muscular spaces with plaster on the weekend he died. DeGraaf did not recognize the type of bird. It was feathered in gold and white.

"A friend sent him the bird from South America," Melanie said. Then she stopped abruptly, as if unsure whether she should have spoken.

DeGraaf nodded. He stared around a few seconds longer, aware that in addition to his feeling that someone had stalked Cotton for weeks or months, he was, within himself, personally afraid of the outcome of the case. He felt cold and the world looked dark.

He shook his shoulders, or perhaps shivered, and turned. "Okay," he said to Melanie. "Let's go back upstairs."

He threw off his feeling of horror, though he blundered into the wine cellar, trying to find his way back to the stairs.

Back in the study, Melanie sighed, the only evidence that she, too, wasn't finding this easy. They finished the sandwiches companionably, without any need for conversation. Finally, around midnight, Melanie's eyes were drooping.

"You're exhausted," DeGraaf said. "It's no wonder, either. You had the funeral this morning, then back to work, then Mrs. Coyne, then your father's office files to search, and now I've put you through this on top of it."

"I simply refuse to hear that. I asked to come along, and none of this is your fault," she said firmly.

"Fault or not, I'm going home now. Get some sleep. I'll pick you up tomorrow morning if you want to go to Rob's office with me. Don't if you'd rather not. You understand that as long as he lets me into his counsel I have a duty to tell him if we find a fact he'd consider important? Would you rather he didn't know you were there when we found the reference to the Johns' baby? Not that

I think he'd tell them—"

"No. I'm not trying to hide anything from them. That's not the point. I just felt that they were too fine to be harrassed. I'd like you to pick me up tomorrow."

They were at my office at ten of nine the next morning. I am not always in so early. It depends on how late I've been kept working the night before. But things were breaking and I hadn't slept.

DeGraaf was punctilious about telling me exactly what he and Melanie had done the day before, including, but not especially emphasizing, the Johns' baby. Melanie sat in a chair biting her lower lip while he did so. For my part, I was just waiting for him to come to the end of it. Possibly I didn't listen so very closely.

When he had finished, I said, "Splendid. I appreciate your keeping me up with all this stuff. Let me tell you what we've been doing here."

DeGraaf immediately gave me one of his narrowed-eye glances and sat down in a chair, lowering himself slowly, as if it might be a trick chair and break away with him. Melanie looked happy— delighted that I hadn't seized up my hat and run out of the office to face her butler and cook and apply thumbscrews to them.

Of the two, DeGraaf knew me better, of course.

"In the last two days," I said, "I have tried everything with those fingerprints. Everything. The national crime center first and also the FBI. Well, neither of them had anything. The prints weren't on file there. Of course, with the FBI you never know. Sometimes they have the prints you're interested in on record but they don't tell you, because the man in question is somebody they're following. Or somebody they're using. They always figure their case is more important than yours, and they make their own rules."

"But that's terrible!" said Melanie.

"It's the way it is. If you find out later and make a stink, they cite national security. To their way of thinking, national security is *them*. Anyway, that didn't work, so I tried BuPers."

"Bloopers?" said Melanie.

"BuPers is the Army Bureau of Personnel. They take the fingerprints of all inductees and all employees too. You know, so that just in case anything happens—"

Melanie broke in, impatiently correcting my euphemistic phrasing. "In case somebody gets blown apart they know who it is." I keep forgetting she's a pathologist and understands that people are destructible. She looks so young. I think it's her vigor that does it.

I said, "Exactly. The thing is, you get a totally different class of prints from BuPers because they aren't criminal. At any rate not necessarily."

"Of course. What did you get?"

"Nothing. They didn't have him, either. That was yesterday's disappointment. So I tried all the local Illinois sources. But that didn't work, so I teletyped the prints around to state files."

"Wouldn't the national files have everything that the state files have?" Melanie asked.

"People always think they have. They *ought* to, but they haven't. States generally don't send prints taken from somebody if the case is dropped early, for instance. And generally they don't bother with trivial offenses. If every time some high school kid is picked up for throwing beer bottles during a basketball game they fired off the prints to the national, they figure they'd be doing nothing but making and sending prints. And on top of that, a lot don't get sent in because of error, or loss, or general laziness."

"Yes, I guess that's always so."

"Melanie, as a pathologist you've taken fingerprints from bodies in order to determine identity, haven't you?"

"Oh, sure. Daily, I would say. It's a standard part of the training. As a matter of fact, we're required to take prints even where the identity of the victim is presumed to be known."

"Have you ever done any work identifying fingerprints?"

"No, we just send them in. I've been meaning to take a course in fingerprints, when I have the chance. I'm still sort of new at the job, though, and I just haven't gotten around to it. I know fingerprints are classified by the types of patterns the ridges form. And I know the eight general types of patterns. But identification is a long study."

"There are two types of plain arches, two types of loops and four types of whorls. The problem of course is that classification is much easier than identification. In the first place, all the five fingers on your left hand, say, are different. To classify the fingers by type, there are standard fixed points of reference that are used all over the world, and standard subdivision into classes and subclasses. There's a mathematical formula for it. But to go beyond that—to show that one print is identical with another, you need an expert to analyze the print for all sorts of tiny characteristics having to do with ridges, and the ends of ridges, and broken ridges and so on.

There are bifurcations where ridges separate, and trifurcations, ridge dots, ridge crossings, enclosures, and so on. Then your expert counts the number of ridge characteristics that are the same in the two prints. These are called points of similarity, and once you exceed a certain number of points of similarity, you presumably have identification. But it all has to be expertly done and it has to be redone for each print that you want to compare your print with and for every single finger. If you find a man's index finger in one place and his ring finger print in another place, you can't be sure they're from the same person unless you have all his prints on file. And naturally if you have only a partial print or a smudged print, you're in trouble."

"Yes. I can see it's more difficult than I thought."

"In a loop type of print, for example, one thing they do is count the number of ridges crossing an imaginary line drawn from the core to the delta.

"People think that a single print found at the scene of a crime is sure to catch the person if his prints are on file, but that isn't true. You can't take a single, unknown print to your main fingerprint files and find out who made it. Not even if it's in there somewhere. The reason for this is that files are classified on the basis of all ten fingers. Some files in major cities—like ours—keep a second classified single-print file. But they only put into it the prints of known repeating criminals like burglars, auto thieves, safecrackers and that sort of thing. People you have a real need to find and people who really might leave a single print at a crime scene."

"But in this case, don't you have all five fingers?"

"Yes, or four fingers and the side of the thumb of a right hand. Okay. So I had people all over the country comparing them to whatever they had. It's very easy to say that one hand did *not* make the prints you have. But going the other way you only have increasing similarity. There has been a lot of testing in the past, as you can imagine, taking prints that were very similar indeed but known to be from different people and counting the points of similarity. The most ever found when the people were different was four points of similarity. Therefore, we generally say that eight points of comparison establish identity."

I was enjoying myself, but DeGraaf wasn't. He stood up, folded his arms and said, "This is enough of your ego trip. I am willing to grant you've been hard at work. But you have no right to keep Melanie in suspense like this. What are you building up to?"

"Who, me?"

"I know you're proud of yourself, but finish the damn story!"

Melanie just stared at us, her brown eyes big, waiting.

"I don't believe Melanie was in suspense," I said. "She doesn't know me as well as you do."

"Lucky Melanie. Go on."

"All right. California finally identified the prints. Fourteen points of similarity on the index finger. The man's been arrested four times for grand theft auto and let go four times for lack of evidence. He's suspected to be tied in with the mob. His name is Clarence Scott."

# CHAPTER TEN

"So you see," I said, "it wasn't a ghost."

"What?" said DeGraaf. "Who said it was done by a ghost?"

"Uh—now that you ask me, I don't know."

"I'll tell you, then. It was you. If I've maintained anything from the start it was that only the people in that room were in a position to kill Cotton. The ghost idea was yours."

"Me? I'm a policeman."

"Sure. And that's exactly why. Faced with evidence—*your* kind of evidence—that no one inside the room touched that knife and that no one outside could have come in, you thought of invisible spirits."

"That's ridiculous. I've said all along that Pryczyk and Johns must have let somebody in. Now we know who. This man Scott could be a hired killer type."

"The reason your mind went to the ghost theory is that all of your training and experience deny that.

Johns isn't at all likely to go into such a thing with Pryczyk or anybody else. Nor both of them with a third party. It's idiotic."

"Idiotic, is it? What do you have to put in place of it?"

"Nothing yet, Rob."

"Well, I have an explanation that will fit the whole thing."

DeGraaf cocked his head at me. I hate it when he does that. Then he said "Oh?" just as slowly as he could.

"Oh, yourself," I said, trying for the Witty Comeback of the Week award. But I was stung. I said, "I have a consistent explanation for the whole thing."

He settled back against the window sill again. "Let's hear it."

"All right, I will. Clarence Scott either hated Cotton or was hired to kill him. At this point it isn't important which."

"Okay. Go on."

"He also knew a lot about him. You agree that whoever killed him knew a lot about him?"

"I will certainly give you that; it's obvious."

"All right. If he knew a lot about him, he knew one simple thing: given Cotton's character, most of the people close to him would have hated him also. Scott disguised himself. Nothing dramatic, just a simple hair rinse, cheek pads and shoe lifts. He cased the place and walked in. Finding Johns and Pryczyk in the hall, he said, 'I'm going to knock off your boss and make your lives easier. It won't be your fault and you won't be blamed. Just stay there and when it's all over swear that nobody went past you. Then he stabbed Cotton and left."

"Why didn't anybody see him?"

"They did. But he wore a dark suit and white shirt that was similar enough to a butler's so that no one was aware of him. Nobody noticed him consciously except Alec."

"Why didn't the door squeak?"

"It did. But the fire was sizzling and popping and no one paid attention."

"Why did he leave his fingerprints?"

"Because it didn't matter. Pryczyk and Johns wouldn't talk and couldn't identify him if they did. Everyone would believe no one had gone in. He probably knew his prints weren't on file in Illinois anyhow. And since there's no particular relationship between Johns and Pryczyk it would be assumed they weren't in collusion. But you and Melanie have given me an additional reason for Johns to hate Cotton. And at that I didn't need it. Pryczyk and Johns had the most important thing in common. They both worked for a bastard."

"And Mrs. Coyne and the bus?"

"She tripped."

I guess I had forgotten Melanie was in the room, I was so intent in shooting down the doubt in DeGraaf's face. I would never have spoken like that about her father if I had remembered she was there.

It took a couple of seconds to hit her, but I became aware she was in the room when she burst out, "That's not true. He was *not* a bastard!"

"I'm sorry," I said, really dismayed. But the damage was done.

"And it isn't true that anybody close to him would have hated him. The Johnses didn't hate him. And Aunt Helen and Alec and I don't—didn't —hate him, either. It just isn't true."

"Of course it isn't," DeGraaf said. But she wasn't going to be pacified that easily.

"I realize he was difficult," she said. "He was picky and he must have been hard to work with at the hospital. But he was a perfectionist and everybody realized that. His job called for perfection. They respected him for it. He was not a bastard."

At that point she burst into tears.

At that point I could have diced my tongue.

Then DeGraaf, perhaps to deflect her thoughts, said, "Robbie, when you get really frustrated with a case you come up with some of the silliest theories the mind of man could create." I wasn't trusting myself, so I kept quiet. "No sane human being walks in front of two unknown men to commit a murder, with or without a wig, when he can pick the man off with a rifle or push him in front of a commuter train. *No one* doesn't care about prints when it's possible and inconspicuous to wear gloves. And on top of that, you've thrown out poor Mrs. Coyne just because she isn't convenient to you. Your eagerness to run up a theory is charming; it's a result of hating to let a mystery ride, I think, and I sympathize. But this particular fiction of yours just won't do. It doesn't make it."

"You don't have any reason to assume Mrs. Coyne was deliberately pushed."

"Look, Rob. There's no point in you and me fighting over this item by item. But I'll challenge you to do one thing: let us into your print lab."

"What for?"

"I want to see whether I can figure out a way to produce prints on that knife. You can have your man hang over me every minute, if you want."

"Sure, he has nothing else to do."

"Like every public department, he has to have slow periods and fast periods. We're willing to wait."

"You would, wouldn't you? You'd sit there and stare at me until I let you in."

"After all, seeing justice done is his first responsibility. And yours."

"Oh, boy. All right. All right. I'll buy it."

Henry Lumpkins is called Humpty Lumpkins by everybody on the force because of his resemblance to Humpty Dumpty. He is egg-shaped. His body is egg-shaped, the lower part a little broader than the narrow shoulders, and his head is egg-shaped too, with a fringe of gray whiskers all along the chin. No mustache, just a one-inch fringe of gray beard. He is also a mass of chuckles. I knew Melanie and De-Graaf would expect our fingerprint expert to look mathematical, probably skinny and dry, with glasses. Humpty listened to their problem and said, "What fun! Let's play around with that weird little knife."

"Scalpel," said DeGraaf.

"Right you are," said Humpty, chuckling.

This business seemed to have helped Melanie. She was not crying any more, though her eyes were puffy. She looked interested. I left her to DeGraaf's care.

"What can you tell us about those prints, Mr. Lumpkins?" DeGraaf asked.

"Variety and vintage," Humpty chuckled. "No, just kidding. It is usually difficult to tell when a print was made. Now plastic prints, which is what we call them when they're left in clay or glue or paint or warm plastic—something that hardens—or some oils, you can sometimes tell the age of the print from the age of the material. But these—not really."

"So you mean they could have been made months ago and left at the scene?"

"Oh, no. Not months. They were still smearable. Body oils will harden over time just like any other oils. They were pretty fresh. Anybody who has lifted prints much can tell that just from the way they pick up the powder. They could have been made an hour before or several days before, though. Except for one thing."

"What?" said Melanie.

"What's that?" said DeGraaf at the same moment.

"They were not smeared, so they were made when the knife was used."

"How can you be so sure?" Melanie asked.

"Look over here. I took several films before we lifted the prints. We wouldn't want that little old defense counsel telling us later that there had never been any prints at all on that knife, would we?" He laughed hugely.

"I guess not," said Melanie.

"See these?" He produced a fistful of glossy black-and-white photographs. The knife, in increasing close-ups, both sides. "See the handle is shiny, and generally clean. A few left-over prints and half-prints I've ID'd as Adam Cotton's. On this side, perfectly clear, are four sets of whorls. On *that* side, towards the top of the knife, half a thumb." On the narrow blade of the knife were stains, blackish in the photograph.

"Now, I'll tell you what I'm going to do," Lumpkins chuckled. "I'll get you a knife with a similar handle—oh, nothing so unusual as that little baby, bladewise, but similar—polished like that, too. One you can play with." He rummaged and rummaged in a drawer that contained old bent wires, pieces of steel, a gate hinge, several pens, and at last, a knife of the sort he wanted.

"Good," said DeGraaf, who had been hoping for just such an experiment.

"Now I'll get some powder. We'll use it in a minute. It'll help you visualize some things. Now, young lady, you pick up the knife and hold it in a natural way."

Melanie did so. She looked pale, but took a breath and then nodded. "I see what you mean," she said. "My fingers fall in just about the same places, with the four fingers on one side sort of low and the thumb on the top of the other side. You think those prints are in a natural position."

"Right you are. Dead on. Oh, that's very good, my dear. Now put it down, that's a good girl. Now I'm just going to blow a little powder over the whole thing. See them better now, don't you?"

"Clear as day," said DeGraaf.

"Okay. Now you," he turned to DeGraaf, "pick up that knife and push it into something. Heh, heh, not me, of course. Stick it into the soil next to this dieffenbachia. Not near the stem, please. Let's not try to kill the poor thing. It's an old friend. Oh, my, yes. Nine years old this one is. Aha! Very good. Now, without messing it around, put the knife down here and look at those prints the pretty lady made."

Melanie and DeGraaf crowded toward it, bumped heads and backed up. Lumpkins giggled happily. They approached again and did it right this time. On the shiny surface of the knife, Melanie's prints were virtually wiped away. Only a few little half-moons of them were left, and against them DeGraaf's prints showed on the handle. His prints were trailed by lines of smudged streaks, where his fingers had slid forward as he pushed the knife in, but all four finger prints were clear. The thumb print, though a little bit farther forward than Melanie's had obliterated hers.

"Yes, I see," DeGraaf said.

"But would that happen if the prints underneath were hardened?" Melanie asked.

"You mean if the lower prints were rather old? Well, not as much. I think they'd still smudge noticeably. Even hardened prints are only comparatively hardened. When they're very old, they're still only oil on shiny, slippery steel. They'd smudge some. And anyway, these weren't. As I told you, these were readily smearable when they got to me. And you can't make 'em hard one day and soft the next. Oh, ho. Oh, my, no. That'd be a lovely trick!"

DeGraaf said, "Well, what if the knife were held some other way?"

"How?"

DeGraaf picked up the knife they'd been playing with, and compared it to the Ferris-Smith scalpel in the picture. The blade was shorter, but the handle and the way the blade was set into the handle were essentially the same. He realized they were not going to give him the actual knife to fool around with, but this was good enough in every way.

He tried holding it with two fingers up near the blade. He couldn't put any force behind it. He tried holding the blade in two fingers and shoving the end of the handle with the palm of his other hand. He was certain from the feel of it there would be no accuracy. Second, he could imagine trying to get hold of it that way with the victim watching. It would be extremely suspicious. Third, try as he would, if he held it long enough to get the blade started into the soil near the plant, his two fingers invariably slipped back toward the handle and left prints. It wouldn't work. Come to think of it, he reflected, the longer the blade, the more it would be inclined to twist when held that way.

"What about some sort of mechanical holder?" he asked.

Lumpkins shrugged, a shrug which ran cheerfully all over his plump body. "There's no part of that knife to get hold *of*," he said. "It's a surgical knife, and it's rounded to fit the hand. Since they are never used in any sort of scabbard or sheath, they're not made with any sort of collar. The place where the tang—that's the part of the end of the blade that goes into the handle—where the tang is inserted is just as smooth as the rest of the thing. Even if you had a holder clamped somehow to a knife with a big cup hilt or a thumb rest or whatever, I don't think it would be very accurate or very practical. But in this case, never. It wouldn't hold."

"Yes. And this was an accurate crime," DeGraaf said. "The right place in the skull, and very quick."

"Surely. And I would hate to try to sneak up on somebody with a knife in a big ugly holder of some kind. The more hardware you add to a thing like this, the more warning you give."

"And the more likely somebody else will see and get suspicious."

"Also," said Lumpkins, "this sort of knife is just

too shiny to be used that way. A metal holder would scratch it. A leather or plastic holder, in fact any soft holder, would leave smudges of its own, plus smudges on the prints underneath. If you'll look at these glossies, you'll see that the places that Cotton's prints have been rubbed off, the new prints have gone over them. There just aren't any of the hard, sharp marks that you would associate with a holder. I wouldn't waste a lot of time on that idea."

"All right, then, what about faking prints on your own hand?"

"What kind of thing do you mean?"

"Oh, I saw a spy movie once that showed little pieces of what looked like polyethelene film being glued to a man's fingertips. It was supposed to give him another man's prints."

"Ha! Fiction! I love it! Let me tell you, there are problems with that sort of thing."

"I felt there would be. Like what?"

"Edges! Wrinkles! If anybody with experience looks at a print made that way—"

"And you have experience."

"You bet your insufflator. Anybody who had seen a lot of cases come and go would be able to tell. Now one way you might get away with it is this: you glue a false print to your fingertip. At the outside edges it will wrinkle and fold, naturally. And at the very edge it will show—well, *edges*. But if you were to touch your finger very, very lightly to a good surface, not pushing down hard enough to cause wrinkles in the polyethelene film, or to bring the outside edge in contact with the surface, you might leave a very deceptive print indeed."

"What you're saying is we haven't got that situation."

"Better believe it. Oh, not by a long shot. These fingers held and pushed hard. And all five of 'em. You can see where they slid forward because of the pressure required to push the knife through the bone of the skull. But when they released they left beautiful prints. There are no edges and no wrinkles, even where you see the *side* of the thumb."

"I admit an experienced person has a sense of when something is real—"

"And if that much doesn't convince you, let me lay this on you. In this case you have as well as fingertip prints, the prints of the ridges of the insides of the fingers. See them there, where they curved around the bottom of the knife? And on the right side of the knife—the right as it would be to you when you held it—you have a fine, clear area of the inside of the palm."

"And no wrinkles?"

"There are the large, one might say fat, normal wrinkles. Look at your own hand and fold it. On a print they show up as areas that fade out to no print and then fade in again across the clear area. You can't make that kind of thing with polyethelene film. It's too thin and too pliable. You'd get flat folds. One area would end abruptly and the next start with hardly any area left clear. Like it was cut off; you get me?"

"Yes, I do. Unfortunately. What about palm prints?"

"What about 'em?"

"Do you take them?"

"I'm not sure what you mean. We don't take them routinely on arrested persons. They aren't on the regular fingerprint cards, you know. There are just spaces for each finger. Like this." He held out a card. It was about eight by eight inches. A row of boxes across the top held spaces for the five fingers of the right hand, rolled. A row of boxes across the middle held the five fingers of the left hand, rolled. In the bottom space were places for the four fingers taken simultaneously, unrolled, the left in a box to the left, the right hand in a box on the right. In the center were the two thumbs, not rolled, and a small box with the terse words, "note amputations."

"No palms," said Lumpkins, chuckling.

"But you use palmprints, don't you?"

"Oh, sure. If there's a palmprint at the scene of a crime and we can match it to a suspect we have in hand, we're glad to get it. Especially if we can't find any good fingerprints."

Melanie asked, "They're equally distinctive, aren't they?"

"As distinctive as fingerprints," DeGraaf said.

"Right you are, and as admissable in court," said Lumpkins. "The first palm print was admitted in the State of Nevada v. Kuhl in 1918. And as they say in showbiz, they never looked back. In People v. Atwood in 1963 the court explicitly stated that palmprint evidence is as admissable and as conclusive as fingerprint evidence."

DeGraaf was staring into space, thinking. Then he asked, "What if we found that the palmprint on our knife was made by somebody who didn't make the fingerprints? Then would you believe the fingerprints were fake?"

"No. I'd rather think I was cracked. But you won't find that. I have had twenty-seven years of working with fingerprints. The knife shows the touch of one hand—better say firm grasp—and it was properly placed to do the damage it did. And

I'll bet my Leica that the palm belonged to the same person who owned the fingers."

"Robert," said DeGraaf. "It isn't much to ask. And won't it look nice anyway, if you're thorough?"

"It isn't *necessary*," I said. DeGraaf was looking strained, which wasn't his style. Normally you've never seen such a happy man. I thought he was grasping at straws.

"Just do it for me," he said. "Think of how much it will support your point of view. It'll take a man a couple of hours at most to get everybody's palm-prints. If you want to keep it to a minimum, just do the right hands."

"But there's no point in it."

"Look, if the palmprint doesn't belong to anybody who was inside that room the night of the bridge party, I'll—I'll admit it's Clarence Scott's palm, even though you don't have his on file. How's that for a handsome offer?"

"Oh, jeez, it'll take me less time to send Turgid out than to argue with you. Go away and I'll send him. Now I've got work to do."

"I can take a hint. I'm going to drop Melanie at her house. She's just about exhausted. I'll be at the hospital later. You can get me there if you want."

"I should want?"

Melanie said, "I'm not so tired, really."

"It's been a terrible four days for you," DeGraaf said. "There's nothing wrong with admitting you're tired."

"All right. I'll go home today, but tomorrow I'm going back to work."

It was late afternoon and the shifts were chang-ing. The hospital had a spurious bustle, one not related to patient care but to comings and goings. De-Graaf shrugged his way through it.

When he reached Mrs. Coyne in intensive care, he stood still and looked at her. Her private nurse stared at him. The nurse in charge of intensive care had come out of her glass cubicle to check a feeding line and she, too, glanced his way. He raised his eyebrows. She shook her head. That was all.

DeGraaf went on to his office, which was actually only a desk in the emergency wing. He found he could not sit. Gringo was on duty and it was, strictly speaking, DeGraaf's day off, but he followed Gringo around while two diabetic comas were admitted, one after the other. He looked over Gringo's shoulder and coached for five or six minutes. Finally Gringo said, "Look. Get out of my way. Either go take care of the next patient or run your head into the wall and stitch it back up."

This seemed to mean he was not wanted there, either, so he went out and took the next patient. It was a simple laceration. A forty-eight year old carpenter, who had been hurrying to get a sheet of plywood cut before five o'clock, had cut a deep gash with a circular saw on the inside of his left forearm.

"I keep telling the kids who come on, don't ever hurry with power equipment," the man said sheepishly.

"Human nature," said DeGraaf. "Shows you're just a kid yourself. Will you move this finger for me please? This one. Now clench the whole hand. Open and make a fist. Do you feel this? And here. You feel that, too? I'm going to numb this and then stitch it. There aren't any major arteries cut here, or any important nerves. You'll be using this arm tomorrow. I'd prefer you didn't play football with it for ten days or so. When you take a shower, keep the stitches as dry as possible. Your own doctor should take the stitches out in about seven days."

DeGraaf found the mechanical job of stitching soothing. It required accuracy, but freed his mind, which he felt had been jumpy and nonproductive. Afterward, when the man had left, he walked away from the wing altogether and ended up, without having thought much about it, on the surgical recovery corridor where there was a chance he would find a certain resident.

His luck was in. Jimmy Ho, the resident in question, emerged from a ward a few doors ahead. He looked angry. DeGraaf didn't pause for that.

"What's the trouble, Jimmy?"

"Oh, hi, Gerritt." Jimmy lowered his voice. "We lost one."

"Oh. I see. Would it make you feel any worse to talk with me for a few minutes about something completely unrelated and confidential?"

"No worse, no better." But he smiled. "Will you step into my linen closet?"

"Delighted."

With the door closed, Ho asked, "What is it, Gerritt? Cotton?"

"Right. Well, only indirectly. Not Cotton; Coyne and Passim."

Ho whistled. "I thought they were all clear. I heard that the fingerprints weren't theirs."

"How news travels. The whole situation is much more complicated than that, although it's true as far as it goes. What about Coyne and Passim? How did they feel towards Adam Cotton?"

"I suppose you really need this? I have an aversion to gossip."

"Yes. I really need it."

"Cotton felt that Passim wasn't fast enough. Whenever Passim had to do part of a procedure, he seemed to take forever. He didn't really, of course. He was learning and trying to be careful, bless him. And Cotton's snide remarks made it worse; anyway, Passim would get so afraid of doing something wrong that he'd think three times before he tied a stitch. Cotton, of course, was trained in the days when anesthesia was less reliable and it was hard to keep a surgical patient stable. He was trained to get in and get out as fast as he could, consistent with doing the job."

"So he was dissatisfied with Passim. But was he going to do anything about it?"

"I don't think so. Cotton had some complaint about every student that passed through his hands. Some worse than Passim, too. You know Cotton."

"He wasn't going to have him dismissed?"

"No—" He hesitated.

"No but what?"

"I'm just not sure that Passim would have realized that."

"I see. All right. What about Coyne?"

"Well, Liam drinks."

"I figured. He drinks at dinner and probably afterward. But does he drink on the job?"

"Absolutely not. He has *never* come in to surgery drunk and he *never* drinks during the day. No martinis at lunch, or anything."

"So what was the problem?"

"Cotton was head of the department. He said Coyne was developing tremors from boozing in the evening. He also said what if one of Coyne's patients needed him in the night and he was too stewed to cope."

"Was he really developing tremors? Did it show during surgery?"

"Not that I could see, and I looked. I figured sooner or later I was going to have to stick my neck out to defend Coyne."

"Why would you do that?"

"He's good at his job. If you threw out every doctor who drinks, or takes drugs, or messes up his health in some way or other, you couldn't begin to handle the patients. We've got a shortage of physicians as it is. Besides, there's plenty of time to catch Coyne later, if he gets worse. Alcohol is a very slowly progressive thing."

"But Cotton wanted to keep him from working here?"

"Yes. Or at least he spoke as if he did."

"Had he ever gone after anyone before, like that?"

"Oh, yes. He had a man dismissed four years ago. It was a worse case. He actually operated drunk one morning. The nurse caught on right away and some orderlies carried him off. The assistant surgeon and nurse had to finish the procedure. That was worse, of course—"

"But Coyne would have to know, because of it, that Cotton could be serious."

"Cotton said that should never happen again."

"So why would Coyne want to go to Cotton's for dinner?"

"Well, knowing how Liam's mind works, I could make a guess."

"Guess away."

"He would go to show Cotton what splendid control he had over liquor. My guess is he would intentionally have two or three drinks during the evening and carefully not have too many. Not enough even to show. Am I right?"

"Bullseye. Up until Cotton turned up dead, after which Liam seems to have tossed back a couple more." DeGraaf reached for the door. "Thanks Jimmy."

"Do I get to know what damage I've done?"

"As soon as I know."

DeGraaf, now very disturbed, wandered down to the cafeteria and picked up a sandwich, not aware of what the filling was. People who knew him did not speak because they could tell from his eyes that he didn't see them. At one point he was standing dazed in the corridor near pediatrics and was run into by a gurney pushed by an intern. Later he sat in a waiting room with a lot of patients' relatives; he drank milk through a straw.

After a time, he went back to the intensive care corridor to make sure Mrs. Coyne was still adequately guarded. This was just an expression of nerves, since the nurse on duty monitored her continually and could see her through the glass of the booth. In addition, the nurse he had asked Liam to request still sat next to the bed.

DeGraaf went back out toward the elevators, not much happier, and just at the edge of his vision thought he saw Alec Spruance turning the corner into a long corridor to his left. He swung around and was fairly sure it was Alec, but the boy disappeared around the corner. DeGraaf called "Alec!" and started to run.

He ran into the second corridor. At the far end two elevator doors were closing. Beyond that there was an open stairway. DeGraaf decided it was hopeless. He could always see the boy later and ask him what he had been doing there. Slowly, he went back to his desk.

He had just reached it when I called him.

"What news, Robert?" he asked, sounding very gloomy. I hardly wanted to give him another disappointment.

"Well, we finished with your damn palmprints," I said. "All except for Mrs. Coyne. It seems the bandage from her broken arm runs down over her palm and back up again."

"I suppose it would. What did you find out?"

"That we shouldn't have bothered. Leaving out Mrs. Coyne, none of our bridge players made the palmprints on that knife. I told you so."

# CHAPTER ELEVEN

"Hell," said DeGraaf.

"So your theory is shot. It's not that serious."

"My theory, as a matter of fact, is not shot."

"Oh?" I suppose I sounded skeptical.

"Never mind."

"Never mind, nothing! Are you telling me you have a theory as to who killed Cotton?"

"Of course I'm saying that. Haven't you been listening?"

"And it's different from mine?"

"I'm afraid so. Yours isn't a theory anyway. It's a fictional hash."

"Who?"

"Robert, come on. I said it's a theory. I want to look into a few things first. People could be hurt."

"Okay. What's the difference? You're wrong anyway, if you really have any notion at all. Carry on in your hopelessly misguided mission." With which rounded phrase, and slightly out of breath, I hung up.

DeGraaf stood up reluctantly and headed himself toward the top floor where the computer terminals were housed. It was now eight in the evening and the people who helped punch cards to ask the computer questions had long since gone home. However, the unit would still respond if given a valid identification number and the correct retrieval codes. DeGraaf hated picky tasks like punching cards, where every single punch had to be right or the card was worthless and you had to reject it and start over. He had long since forced himself to learn the system, though.

The punch was a keyboard resembling a typewriter, set into a console that fed cards as needed. It stood on the floor in a row of six others of its kind, with its own attendant swivel chair. On the near wall was a bin with rows and rows of cards with various colored stripes running down the tops. The cards were about three inches by eight. DeGraaf seized a block of the ones with yellow stripes and put them into the hopper to feed. With a nice little hum the first card moved across the feeding line, unhurried, into the place in front of the punch. DeGraaf punched his job card, his program card, and began.

Thirty minutes later he had the full hospital record on Jimmy Wigoda and Aileen Lee. Translated from the shorthand:

Wigoda had been a night watchman in a large pickle factory. One night three boys had broken in, intending to steal a barrel of pickles and dump them on the porch of a friend. Wigoda had surprised them in the act of rolling a large crock of pickles onto a dolly. Two had punched him, but one had hit him on the head with another stoneware crock. He was found in the morning, unconscious, and taken to Hastings Hospital. The diagnosis was subdural hematoma, skull fracture, and injuries to the brain. He never regained consciousness, but lay, fed and maintained by machine, for twenty-seven weeks before he died. Death was due to kidney failure which would not respond to dialysis, and a respiratory infection. Out of all the medical personnel who had seen Wigoda in that time, one was a name that mattered: Peter Erikson had supervised the dialysis. Not that there was anything unusual about that. At Hastings he would have been the natural person to have done so. There was no hint of any mistake. According to the record, nobody had pulled the plug on the man. There was no hint of misjudgment in all the long medical record of Wigoda's hospitalization. A man who had had no brain activity for nearly seven months, and who was using thousands of dollars worth of equipment and hundreds of personnel-hours, had died in generally the way that might have been expected. No wonder Cotton had used the case to support his argument.

Aileen Lee was a bit different. A young woman, twenty-six years old, she had entered the hospital because a serious fall in her home had injured an artery in her leg. After some observation and an angiogram, the opinion was that she would lose her lower leg unless the artery were patched, the damaged section replaced by silastic tubing.

The artery was duly repaired, but during surgery she had a reaction to the halothane they were using as an anesthetic. In spite of being continuously ventilated, she went into cardiac arrest. This was reversed, but she never pulled out of the coma. It was no fault of the surgeon, nor of the anesthesiologist. There was no advance indication that she might not tolerate halothane. All the usual standards had been adhered to—as far as the record showed. She lived three months on machines and succumbed to a sudden fulminating respiratory infection. Autopsy showed, in addition to necrotic areas in the brain, some in the liver as well, confirming an idiosyncratic reaction to halothane. Her surgeon had been Dr. Liam Coyne.

DeGraaf sighed. He had absolutely no reason to think that anybody had been at fault in either death, so why should anybody be sensitive to references to them? Well, he did not know that anyone had been. In fact, Cotton's manuscript had never gone beyond the assertion that the best medical opinion at the outset considered both cases incapable of recovery. Indeed, this was Cotton's point. The two patients then consumed huge quantities of skilled care and equipment. Cotton had not suggested anything fishy about their deaths.

All right. But was the audience that night to know what Cotton would say in the paper? If someone felt guilt, if someone had made a mistake and covered it carefully, or had pulled a plug at the family's request, such a person could not very well go up to Cotton and ask to check over his manuscript. He would have to assume, given Cotton's needling, self-important character, that he was being told his secret would come out in print. And hearing that the manuscript was unfinished, he could kill Cotton and be certain the paper would never be published.

And if that were so, why not throw the manuscript in the fire? That was easy. First, the flare of brighter flames would attract the attention of everybody in the room. Even two or three pages would burn far more brightly than the wood. Second, the killer would face the problem of spending time looking through the manuscript for the right pages, an awkward and attention-getting move, every moment raising the chance of discovery. Third, burning one or two pages could only attract attention to the manuscript if anyone paged through it. Since Cotton could easily have a carbon copy or an early draft somewhere else a move like that would be stupid. Better to pretend that the manuscript lying there had nothing to do with the killing. Chances were that, appearing irrelevant, it wouldn't even be read. If it were, at least there would be no missing pages to attract attention. And as for any references to anyone in the room, the killer had a good response: it was just another of Cotton's continual efforts to show that nobody knew anything but himself.

DeGraaf was beginning to hate this case. He no longer wanted to be involved. His head ached and his wits felt dulled.

The computer terminal room was too cold. His feet and hands were chilled. Or maybe it was fear. He had turned on the light only over the punch at which he sat and all the reaches of terminals and tables beyond were shrouded in darkness. He sighed again and his sigh was lost in the dark edges of the place. DeGraaf stood up, sweeping his papers into a rough pile.

The room swayed before him. He closed his eyes for a minute. He was in that state where he needed sleep but knew it would be impossible. Every sense was on edge, but too highly keyed up to be accurate. As he swung his head, a couple of the punch machines at the outside of his vision seemed to tilt away from him.

DeGraaf walked quickly to the glass door. Shoving it open with the elbow of the arm that held the papers, he made it into the hall. As soon as he did so, he became aware of thinking in those terms and was ashamed of himself. "Made it into the hall," indeed. He wasn't being pursued, nor was he sick. At worst he was tired and badly worried. That was all.

Still the empty corridors in the night had an effect on the nerves. The absence of visitors, cleaning people, and wagons with food trays left the corridors vacant, and gusts of pain and fear and death shrieked down the empty spaces. There was too much emotion in a hospital at any time, but you noticed it at night in the absence of errands and bustle. Somewhere, always, patients were awake and fearful. Death walked here. People cried out for something to stop pain. All the sorrows of life were crowded together in a hospital.

DeGraaf prowled, looking while walking for something other than the idea in his mind. He went down the circular stairs from the computer terminals on the top floor—all the way across the hospital, from west to east, on the third floor level. Through the surgical corridors to the bridge, from this building across the night to the doctors' building, a shaft of glass in a void.

Coyne's office was in back on the third floor. No one else was in, but fluorescent light burned in the empty hall. DeGraaf's feet fell quietly on tan carpeting.

There was Coyne's door, and a light behind the glass. He knocked.

"Who's that?" Coyne sounded afraid.

"Gerritt DeGraaf, Liam. May I come in?"

"Oh. Oh, sure." There was a thump like a chair overturning on carpet, a rustle of paper, some fumbling with the door, and in ten seconds more Coyne had the door open. He was rumpled, as if a huge hand had tried to wad him up and throw him away. His shirt collar was open and his eyes were red. He smelled of whiskey.

"Come in," he said. "You didn't bring bad news?"

"Oh, lord, no."

Coyne fumbled his way back to his swivel chair. The desk in front of it was strewn with twisted paper clips, open newspapers, and a glass. There was a half empty bottle on the typing table. Several books were lying around on the floor, the table, the second chair. DeGraaf saw that they were all on brain trauma.

DeGraaf took the chair that the patient would usually sit in. "How was she when you last heard?" he asked.

"Unchanged. Damn unchanged."

"So that means no worse."

"No, no. Brain activity. But what if she wakes up brain damaged? Or palsied. She'd be so ashamed to look incompetent. Brain things are hellish. Unpredictable. What if she develops pneumonia? God knows what?"

"Liam, how do you think the accident happened?"

"How the hell can I know?"

"I mean, what do you guess about it? Do you believe she saw the murderer? At Cotton's that night?"

"You mean the murderer pushed her in front of the bus?" Coyne looked at him with such amazement in his face that DeGraaf was shocked. Mentally, he staggered. Coyne was an intelligent man.

How was it possible that he had never considered this before? There was only one explanation.

"Was it your idea that she just fell?" DeGraaf let it hang.

"Uh—I suppose so," Coyne said. "I hadn't thought about it, exactly."

"Liam, did Cotton have it in for you?"

"Yeah, I guess he did. He was the watchdog of the world. He had the idea that because I take a couple of drinks with dinner I'd be no good for the next day."

"I doubt if he was right about that."

Coyne half smiled. "I doubt it too. Cotton, of course, didn't go in for doubts. Anyway, he didn't have any support in his position, so it wouldn't have mattered."

"It was embarrassing, I'm sure."

"Are you suggesting that *I* killed him?" Coyne asked completely without heat.

"No, I'm not. But you know, if the person who killed Cotton pushed your wife in front of the bus, I should think you'd like to know, too."

"I'd like to know," Cotton said tiredly, "but I haven't the energy to try to find out." But he said it like a man who had no need to find out.

"Would Cotton have got Passim out of here?"

"That kid? No. Cotton always bitched about students. He figured people ought to be born with twenty years of experience, as no doubt he believed he was.

"Yes. Okay. Did Passim think Cotton might get rid of him, though?"

"I don't think so. Come on, don't blame it on him, Gerritt. He didn't kill Cotton. And whoever did—wasn't all bad."

●　●　●

I was waiting at DeGraaf's desk when he got back
from seeing Coyne. He walked in rubbing his eyes,
looking tired. It was just past midnight.

"I've been talking with Coyne," he said, showing
no surprise at seeing me there and without asking
what I wanted. I knew immediately he was worried.
But if he was worried, I was terrified and I had
something to tell him.

"Oh, that's nice," I said.

"Rob, that man believes his wife killed Cotton to
protect him. He must have talked at home about
Cotton thinking he drank too much. Mrs. Coyne
must have suggested trying to get an invitation to
Cotton's party, or he wouldn't be so scared. He
thinks she stabbed Cotton and then threw herself in
front of a bus."

"Silly ass," I said. "The fingerprints alone rule
that out."

DeGraaf went on as if he hadn't heard me. "I
went to him to talk about the Aileen Lee business
and I was so stunned I completely forgot to mention
it. I asked a few things about stuff I already knew,
so as not to run out into the hall immediately. But
Rob, what an absolutely crushing burden for Coyne
to have on his mind!"

"What Aileen Lee business?" I tried to show
some interest, figuring it was better to let DeGraaf
get this stuff off his chest first. Before I told him
what I had.

"One of the two deaths mentioned in Cotton's
manuscript. I pointed the manuscript out to you."

"Oh, yeah."

He told me the whole story of Aileen Lee and of
Jimmy Wigoda, the older man, too. He pointed out

several places where an error could have been made and ways in which a machine could be turned off, then restarted, and nobody the wiser.

"That's interesting," I said finally.

"Say, what's the matter with you, tonight, Rob?"

I shivered, and he saw it. He was right, all right; there was something the matter. Now that I had his attention, it was time to tell him.

"I found a report on my desk when I got back from dinner."

"Yes?"

"It was in response to inquiries I had been sending out. I'd been trying to find out whether Clarence Scott had been seen around the Chicago area lately."

"All right. And so?"

"He wasn't in any of our current files, you see. But somebody in one of the precincts remembered and checked back."

"Come on, Rob."

"Clarence Scott died eight months ago. He was drowned, by himself or maybe by the mob, in Lake Michigan, just off the pier near Belmont. That's maybe six blocks from Cotton's home. Cotton was stabbed by a dead man."

# CHAPTER TWELVE

A prehistoric terror entered the room then, or perhaps I had been carrying it around with me all night. I could imagine the man Scott, hating Cotton, going down in the icy waters of the lake, surfacing the last time and fixing his eyes on the lighted windows of Cotton's mansion. I imagined him cursing Cotton for some evil done him in the past, cursing him as his mouth filled with water and his breath smothered, then rising, months later, a vengeful spirit from the grave, entering the library through the open window. A vapor would eddy past, unseen by the card players. That dead, invisible hand would take up the knife and kill the man it hated.

And leave fingerprints? Well, if spirits could move knives, they could leave fingerprints. It was all nonsense. I told myself that over and over. It was definitely all nonsense.

If I felt it, the superstitious horror, I soon was aware that DeGraaf felt it too. I looked at him and he was gray, his lips tight and a kind of dread upon his face. DeGraaf is not like that. He is more apt to laugh than to groan. But he groaned then, and shivered as I had.

"Oh, God," he said, "it's just as bad as I was afraid it was."

And I had hoped he would tell me it was nonsense.

I wanted nothing so much right then as a crowded bar and a lot of people talking loudly. I knew I was being silly, and all I needed was an environment that would make me believe it as well.

As if reading my mind, DeGraaf said, "Let's go to Ernie's and have about six beers."

Once DeGraaf suggested something like that, he always went into action immediately. I followed him. I had to: I needed leadership.

Ernie's was one of those places that has driven up the price of stained glass for the rest of us mortals. But cheerful was the word. DeGraaf had picked right.

There was a loud hand at the piano bar, but good, and he was in the middle of a Scott Joplin retrospective. The other bar, the one with the brass rail and the pre-Chicago-fire oak top, was absolutely jammed. I hadn't seen so many people in a bar since St. Patrick's Day. DeGraaf stood behind the other customers, who were lined up four-deep. He waved his arms over his head as if he were calling an extra point kick, and yelled at the bartender, "Hey Tukey! Four beers!"

"Hey, hatchet-man! Coming up!"

The other people holding up the bar stared at DeGraaf, who smiled pleasantly. They figured he was a contract killer. But I, thinking swiftly, deduced that the bartender was referring to DeGraaf's profession. We had the four beers in record time, the people at the bar backing away when DeGraaf went in to seize them. Don't make a killer mad.

We found a small round table not too near the Nebraska egg-packers' convention, or whatever it was that was keeping the part of the room under the art deco nude in jolly condition.

"Hey, Gerritt," I said, "the cognoscenti never order four beers for two people. It gives the fizzies a chance to escape in the second drink."

"The way I feel it won't have a chance to. Do you have the gall to claim you don't feel the same way?"

"Mmm. I couldn't quite claim steady nerves, that's true."

"And anyway, if you're going to get cranky, you can fight your way in for our second round."

"I was going to anyway," I said with dignity. "I consider it my duty."

Well, there were no ghosts here. It was too loud. If you expired in this place, no one would find you until sweeping-up in the morning, when they'd rake you out with the peanut shells. We had lights, sound, and beer. DeGraaf plied me with beer.

He didn't talk business, either—until, about two, he steered me out the door and we stood waiting on the curb, ready to trap the first cab that came by.

"Robert," he said, "Hangover or no hangover, you realize that first thing in the morning you have to rush over and get an exhumation order."

Now is this anything to say to a man whose stomach is already three parts awash?"

"What for?" I said sullenly. "They'll want a good reason."

"Dear friend, you are totally confused. A dead man cannot have reached out to kill Cotton."

"My God, yes," I said, my stomach doing a lurch. "I wasn't thinking! *Who is buried in Clarence Scott's grave?*"

"Good boy! And if that's not enough, you're also investigating a major felony, connected—"

"Connected with the man who is supposed to be buried there. We have a killer roaming around and a falsified burial. That should be plenty of reason for an exhumation order."

"Certainly. Get it first thing in the morning and try to schedule it for early afternoon. One o'clock would be good."

"Right after lunch. That'll be nice."

"You are a killjoy. Have the original autopsy report with you, too. I'm going to bring a friend."

"Oh?"

He sighted a cruising cab and yelled and waved his hand. The cab responded. DeGraaf boosted me into it and gave the driver my home address, as if I were incompetent.

"Aren't you coming too?" I asked.

"Not right now," he said. He slammed the door. When I looked back he was already lost in an early morning mist. Believe it or not, I fell asleep on the way home.

What DeGraaf did with the rest of the night, I do not know. He never told me. But when I got to his desk at eleven with the papers, feeling like his personal retriever, he looked like old man death himself. He glanced through the papers quickly and without much apparent interest. Then he took me to a small room and fed me coffee and doughnuts while he stared at the wall. Usually he has the appetite of a grizzly just out of hibernation. I didn't understand his behavior.

Outside, it looked like rain. I just love a rainy exhumation.

"I hope it rains," DeGraaf said.

"Let's go," he announced at eleven forty-five. Then the phone rang.

He picked it up. "Oh, Melanie. Sure," he said. He paused. "Sort of. I won't be able to until later, though. Are you going to be there all afternoon?" Another pause. "Fine. I've got to do something, but I would rather you didn't come. I'll catch you later on. Goodbye."

He picked up his coat. I was standing waiting.

I followed him again through corridors, not knowing where we were going until, suddenly, we opened a door and there was the corridor of people hitched up by vein to machines. DeGraaf, nodding at patients right and left, found the room where Erikson had been last time. He was there again. He looked up and saw us. He didn't exactly go white as paper, but there was a definite look of strain. Altogether, he seemed older than before, too. I doubt that he had been having a good week.

DeGraaf perched on a table, uninvited. I stood by, knowing when to be quiet.

"Um, Peter," DeGraaf began, wiping his eyes, "how are things?" To me, this sounded inane.

"Oh, all right," Erikson said, "considering."

"You know that manuscript of Cotton's?"

"Sure I do. Did you know I had one of those cases he was talking about? Nothing we could do for him."

"Yup. I don't think taking the manuscript out of

the study after Cotton died would have helped at all.

"Oh. Maybe that's just as well."

"Peter, have you had any ideas about getting away from here for a while? A little vacation, something like that?"

Erikson stared at him. No wonder. Slowly he said, "No. There had been some talk of a wedding trip, of course."

"Yes, I know. Peter, do you have some spare time right now? Say an hour or a little more?"

"Right now? What for?"

"Right now. I'd like to show you something."

Erikson looked at me, looked back at DeGraaf, and fixed his gray, strained, handsome face into an expression of pleasant interest. "I can get someone to cover for me for a while, I suppose," he said. "We've done our blood. Actually, the nurses are able to handle it if the resident's on call." He punched a button and a box on the table squawked. He said, "Henry? Are you going to be around? I have to go out for an hour or two." The box made another noise, but Erikson no doubt got the message, because he thanked it and started to take off his white coat.

"It's going to rain soon," said DeGraaf helpfully, as three of us stood watching the grave diggers.

Erikson had not once asked what we were doing here. Not once. All he said was, "Shouldn't we help them? It's heavy work."

"Not on your life," I said. "They're union and there'll be hell to pay if we do."

That was the total extent of the conversation which occupied the entire half hour while the spades dug into the clay. DeGraaf stared at the clouds, which were building up into fat, muddy mushrooms over the city. It was just about bump and scrape time down in the hole when the skies let loose. Raindrops thwacked into the clay and little rivers of green-gray mud started running into the grave.

"Good thing we expected this," DeGraaf said. He added, to Erikson, "We figured that if it rained, we'd take the coffin direct to the medical examiner's lab."

I stared at him fuzzily, knowing that we'd planned to take it there all along. There was a time when coffins were brought up, taken into a tent next to the grave site, and samples taken on the spot so that the coffin could be immediately reinterred. Lately this has been considered old-fashioned. I surely didn't know what DeGraaf was talking about, but with the cursing of the gravediggers, who were slipping in water and mud, and the cold rain down my neck, I was in no mood to bandy chitchat. Then DeGraaf saw the second gravedigger, just lifting the coffin, slip backwards in the water and mud. The man lost his grip on the coffin and in an instant more it would have crashed down on his foot or leg. But DeGraaf seized the end of it, gave it a terrific pull, wrenching it from the grasp of the gravedigger in back, and slipped it up onto the sod. There were no union objections.

The trip to the morgue was drippy and silent.

We pulled into the basement of the ME labs in the car. That's how it's set up. By hearse or car, you can drive into the building only underground. No doubt this is to spare the taxpayers sight or reminders of mortality. That afternoon the taxpayers were very lucky indeed. Out of their sight four soaked and muddy men scrambled from a long car, two of them, DeGraaf and Erikson, looking half dead. Then we slid out onto a trolley one utterly mud-soaked coffin. We trundled it along the glazed white floor with a rubber-tired rumble, dripping mud and water after us so that the hall looked as if a long-dead dinosaur had struggled up out of the ooze.

"Let's try three," DeGraaf said. For a second I didn't understand him. Then I recalled he worked here, part of the time, and must be referring to a room that was likely to be empty.

It was. Maybe it was not used because it was so small. It was then that I found out DeGraaf had a crowbar. And a screwdriver. Probably we could have got some from a supply case in the building, but it was nice that he had planned ahead.

The coffin screws shrieked, unwilling at first to be unscrewed. They had been buried eight months. I waited for my stomach to go into another agony with the sound, but I found that I was inadvertently watching Erikson, instead of the coffin.

DeGraaf had the lid unscrewed. Erikson looked carved from stone and just as cold. DeGraaf seized the whole lid and wrenched it up and off, stepping back quickly. He told me later you step back quickly in case of "gases" escaping. In one smooth motion, we laid the lid against the wall.

Peter Erikson stepped forward and looked at the body in the coffin. As I watched, he turned white as bone, his eyes went up in their sockets until they disappeared, and he fainted dead away.

DeGraaf had anticipated this. He caught Erikson

as he fell and lowered him gently to the floor, his hand under Erikson's head. Then he stood up and looked at a place behind me, fearfully I thought. My scalp prickled and I turned around.

Melanie Cotton was there, her eyes wide. She put a hand in her pocket and threw a couple of pills in her mouth.

I stared stupidly at her as her eyes met DeGraaf's. Melanie turned and went to sit down on the bench. After a couple of seconds I think I heard her whisper to DeGraaf, "I might have loved you." Then she leaned over sideways and seemed to have fallen asleep.

"My God!" I yelled. "Call an ambulance! Call a doctor!"

"Yes, do that," DeGraaf said, not moving. "There's the phone. But I'm afraid it's too late."

# CHAPTER THIRTEEN

Melanie Cotton died an hour later without having regained consciousness. DeGraaf left sometime that afternoon while I was busy with details, and I didn't know where he had gone. His friend Gringo claimed not to know either, and would only say he was covering for him and that DeGraaf had frequently done the same for Gringo: including the time when Gringo had tried to push chick peas into his blender by hand and ended up with hummous tartare.

DeGraaf had not stayed even to explain to me how he knew who had killed Cotton. I could imagine what he was feeling, but I was angry just the same. So I left orders for every patrolman on the Rush Street beat to keep an eye on his windows and let me know when he was back. When word came a week later, I made it to his place in seventeen minutes, a record, but since it was past two in the morning, the traffic was light.

He didn't look especially drawn as a result of his

experience here. He claimed to have been in Mexico, learning to dive from very high cliffs into the sea. I knew I would never find out exactly how fond he had been of Melanie Cotton, and anyway I was afraid to ask. But everything else was fair game. I was annoyed.

"You left me holding the bag," I said. "I don't love having to explain to the commissioner how the suspect was able to escape by suicide before my eyes. Or why the case was closed with half the evidence missing."

"Oh, come on," said DeGraaf. "You had the body and the original post mortem report. I don't have to lead you by the hand."

"Of course not. I'm talking about the things you kept from me."

"Nothing. Not a thing."

"Because otherwise, how could you have figured it out while I missed it?"

"That, Robert, I am too polite to say."

He sat perched on a merry-go-round horse, one of four he uses as bar stools. The pole is cut eight inches above the saddle, so it's like a pommel and you can lean on it. He splashed out some whiskey for us both, then leaned his elbow on the thing and cupped his chin in his hands.

"So what did you tell your commissioner?"

"When I saw the corpse and saw that the skin had been stripped from Clarence Scott's right hand and then, in a blinding flash of intelligence, looked at the original post mortem report you had me dig out and saw that Melanie Cotton had been the pathologist, it was fairly clear. *After* the fact."

"There were a lot of early indications. I should have thought of them the night of the murder, if only I had been alert. But there isn't any point in looking backward."

"*What* should you have known the night of the murder?"

"Well, look what we had: a perfect locked-room murder. No one could have gotten into the room from outside, and no one inside could have done the killing, either. But there's a problem with that right away. Only an idiot sets up a locked-room murder. A murderer is not in the business of providing entertainment for police inspectors. He's interested in getting rid of somebody and not getting caught. I suppose you can imagine some psychoses that would drive a man deliberately to make fools of the police that way, but we didn't seem to have any such person. And it would take a lot to convince me that anybody would want to try it."

"How about a policeman who had been dismissed for incompetence—"

"Okay, maybe. But we didn't have one of those, either. The only good reason to produce a 'locked' room is to make the killing look like suicide. But the killer in our case made no effort to do this, either."

"That's obvious."

"And in any case, if we look closer, it's clear that only a chance event made this into a locked-room murder. Pryczyk just happened to come into the hall at the moment that Johns was cleaning the floor. Thirty seconds later Johns would have been gone and Pryczyk, if he had any conversation with the butler, would have had it in the kitchen. You see that?"

"Certainly I see that."

"Well, don't get so testy. I didn't realize it at first. Not as a thing that *meant* something. If the gardener and the butler had not stopped there to talk, we probably would never have solved the case."

"Why?"

"Wait. So nobody tried to set up an impossible situation, then. What *did* the murderer expect to happen? Why simply that a set of prints that didn't belong to anybody in the party would be found on the knife. Maybe the murderer didn't want innocent persons blamed. Anyway, it would be—it would *have* to be—assumed that the killer came from outside. The bridge players would say that they didn't see anybody come in, probably, unless they wanted to make themselves important. But they could not possibly swear no one came in. Because of the nature of the game, no one could watch every minute. And as you yourself mentioned, we would have to assume that the crackling of the fire covered the creaking of the door."

"Why not oil the door?"

"Simple. Johns might notice. Or Mrs. Johns. Probably both of them; they're very alert. They are very good at their jobs. If they happened to mention that the door had been recently and mysteriously oiled, that would instantly turn suspicion back on those inside the house. Not on the guests, but the people who lived there. Even if you count Alec as living there, that would make only five. And that was too small a number. Besides, it would provide the first clue that the outside stranger was not real."

"Say! It was Melanie who told Johns to go take a break while the guests were playing cards."

"Yes, it was Melanie." This was the first time that DeGraaf had spoken her name. I watched his face, but he gave nothing away and after a few seconds went on. "She did not expect anyone to be sitting outside that door all evening long. And of course, she couldn't see through it. So she went ahead. Now, the knowledge that there would be a fire, that there would be bridge, and that the room was set up in such a way that Adam Cotton, not playing, was at one end and the bridge players at another all argued powerfully that the killer was someone who knew the house and Cotton's habits well. That gave us Melanie, Aunt Helen, Alec, and Peter Erikson. It pretty definitely eliminated Passim and the two Coynes, who had never been in the house before, though the Coynes at least knew there would be bridge."

"And the Johnses and Pryczyk."

"No. The prints were put on the knife to show that an outsider, someone *not* in the room, had killed Cotton. It would have been utterly asinine for anyone outside to go to that kind of effort and wind up directing suspicion right out the door at himself. Johns and Pryczyk would have been better off to have Johns enter the room with a bottle of wine, stab Cotton in the course of pouring him a drink, and leave. Naturally, they would have wiped the knife clean of prints. Then they could set up their mutual alibi. At worst they would simply have been two among eleven suspected people. No, the existence of those prints combined with their claim to have been in the hall eliminates them at one swoop."

"But not an impulse killer inside the room."

"Rob, he would have had only his own finger to work with. Either somebody knew the place and the plans and prepared for the fingerprints, or else he would have left his own prints. Not both."

"Okay, okay."

"Another thing we should have noticed right at the beginning: Melanie was the only person with some control of the seating at the bridge tables. She acted as the hostess. Aunt Helen habitually dithered and Alec was not put in charge of anything. Now Melanie, intelligently, did not tell everyone where to sit. She could have, and it would have seemed perfectly natural at the time, but she didn't want it remembered later, just in case. Very careful. By taking Alec as her partner and suggesting that they break up couples, and then herself walking to the chair with the best view of her father, she managed to put the men at the blind table—Coyne, Passim and Erikson. She had kept talking to me off and on, so that I would tend to head toward her table. Then when she saw I was placing my back to the room, which was ideal for her purposes, she suggested that Mrs. Coyne be my partner. This was much better for her than having Aunt Helen in that seat. Aunt Helen might stare around the room and the chair opposite me was the only one other than Melanie's which had a good view. She was betting that Mrs. Coyne, like any really good bridge player, would keep her mind on the game."

"And even at that she saw something."

"Just barely. And she wasn't sure what she saw. Melanie needn't have worried, but by that time the effect of inadvertently having produced a locked room had gotten to her. She had panicked."

"The whole thing was unnecessarily risky."

"I doubt it. Melanie also made certain, by having Alec at our table, that there would be tantrums to further distract us. And the most important thing of all: sooner or later Alec would bid foolishly, whether he had a good or bad hand, out of frustration and a desire to show off. She needed a partner who would bid no matter what the cards, because she *had to be dummy*."

"And while he was playing, you people would be concentrating on beating him too, and not watching."

"Yes; we might even have doubled, considering his style of play, and be particularly determined to set him."

"You had the advantage of me there. I don't play bridge."

"I explained the game to you the first minute I saw you."

"It's not the same thing."

"Robert, do stop complaining."

"Are you telling me those things told you who'd killed Cotton?"

"No, not at all, unfortunately, or I would have known immediately. And been saved a lot of difficulty." That was skirting his problem. "No, but those facts confirmed it later, when I thought back on it. They were general indications that I should have paid more attention to. But there was a specific set of circumstances that made it clear, and made it necessarily Melanie."

"Shoot."

"The prints on that knife. No outsider had entered the room, therefore the prints got on the knife somehow, without Clarence Scott actually being there. That's the mental leap you didn't want to make. It was clear from Lumpkins, your expert, and from simple observation, for that matter, that the prints were genuine in the sense that those fingers and that palm had actually held the knife. Not only held it, but pushed it in, and it had not been touched afterward. How could that be? No one came in the door, no one came in the window, no one hid in the room. Well, the only way to produce real fingerprints is with a real hand or at the very least the skin of a real hand. But that is not an easy thing to find. Who could possibly get such a thing? Not Aunt Helen or Alec or Mrs. Coyne. Not the Johnses or Pryczyk. For any of them to get such a thing, they would have had either to kill for it, literally, or buy it in some way from highly illegal sources. The second method presumes knowledge they *don't* have, and moreover, it would leave a trail. It might even give someone in the underworld a hold over them. The first method, to kill, would make even less sense. You don't take a chance of getting caught for an unnecessary murder to hide a second, desired murder. There are too many easier ways to kill a person. That goes for both methods. No—it had to be someone for whom getting the skin from a human hand was so easy as to be unnoticeable. Safe, simple, and not involving any deviation from his or her normal routine."

"A doctor could get one."

"You might think so, but where? You don't skin your patients and you can't just amputate any passing body. That kind of thing would cause an immediate scandal."

"A body from the medical school, maybe?"

"The cadavers are locked up pretty carefully. They're valuable, for one thing. If one of our bridge players had taught anatomy—maybe then. But except for me nobody was even associated with the medical school. They were practicing physicians—even Passim. And for any of them to break into the school labs at night, for instance, would be extremely dangerous. It's just another case of the solution being more difficult than the original problem. Nor do any of our suspects do post mortems—except Melanie and me. Coyne and Passim are vascular surgeons. If a patient of theirs died, they might watch the post mortem to see why, but they could not run off with a hand. The same goes for Erikson, who doesn't do any surgery at all."

"Yes, okay. I can see that."

"But Melanie and I were different. We had access to unclaimed bodies under circumstances where we were virtually our own bosses. Melanie more often than I because she was a regular employee of the M.E.'s office. I mostly consult on things that look difficult. As a result of that, too, I usually have a few people watching when I work there. Melanie doesn't."

"She often has students."

"And the student often runs out sick, as we saw ourselves, and doesn't come back until it's all over. The day she took the skin, she was either alone or the student left ill."

"All right. So it was you or Melanie."

"I was eliminated in my own mind, of course. But you could have eliminated me too, because the one thing almost everybody agreed upon—everybody at our table—was that I did not get up during the bridge game."

"I never suspected you."

"Of course not, Rob. Well. All Melanie had to do was wait for the right body. A drifter who wouldn't be claimed by anybody. In this case an out-of-state small time criminal. Say, Rob, how come you didn't find his prints here in Illinois right away? He had a record here, hadn't he?"

"That had been retired when he died. They don't

generally expect dead men to go around commit-
ting crimes."

"So Melanie received a body that was not only
going to be buried at public expense, which is to say
without much attention, but had also been in the
water. Now, any skin can be removed and tanned,
as the daughter of a taxidermist would know, but
soaking, if it isn't too long, makes the skin easier to
remove. It loosens it. Maybe she'd been waiting for
such a body, or maybe the body gave her the idea,
just because it was so perfect. Anyway, one incision
down the back of the hand and the deed is done. No
need to disturb the palm or the fingers at all. Later
she would sew up the incision on the back, making
a 'glove.' When she got home, she had all her
father's taxidermy supplies to work with. She must
have been careful not to upset his arrangements,
and not to use much of the chemicals, in case he
missed some. I checked, though, that he kept extra
cans of most things. It wouldn't be difficult if she
were careful, and the thing she had to cure was
small and wouldn't use much. Once she had the
skin like leather, she had only to put it away and
keep it pliable with a little leather softener now and
then. Up to that point she had not really done anything wrong. She hadn't killed anybody. At most
she had tampered with a body, but her work com-
pelled her to tamper with bodies every day, so she'd
hardly think that was much to worry about. Then
she waited for Cotton to suggest a party. Maybe she
was waiting for one that included several people
who disliked her father, just to be on the safe side."

"Wouldn't the people who buried the body have
noticed something was wrong?"

"No. In drowning cases it is often necessary to

amputate one or more fingers to do fingerprint identification. Also, a lot of damage occurs to drowning victims if they're in the water long. The undertakers would assume there was something about the skin of the hand that required further tests, or that the hand had been cut or hit by a motorboat and therefore saved for evidence."

"Okay. It was still risky to do the murder in front of eight people. Seven I mean."

"I don't agree. It is always risky to murder someone when you're the prime beneficiary. This was spectacularly confusing and managed to throw suspicion on the seven other people as well."

"If you say so."

"It confused *you*."

"All right, all *right*."

"She wore pockets that night, do you remember? A denim suit with pockets. She was the only one of the women to do so. Mrs. Coyne had on a straight sheath with no details at all and Aunt Helen wore something filmy and draped. But Melanie wore pockets and she had the tanned skin in the pocket. She probably put it on when she first went over to offer her father more brandy, the first time she was dummy. She couldn't be absolutely sure of getting another chance. The skin would be like a glove, with the nails missing, of course. That wouldn't matter because the nails wouldn't have been expected to come in contact with the knife anyway. She put the 'glove' on, and maybe rubbed her hand through her hair a moment to pick up oils and make the prints clearer. Then she picked up her father's scalpel and stabbed him, probably at the time when she offered him brandy. We heard him grunt something and she poured an inch of brandy in his glass.

Quite a good cover. Then not sure whether everybody would be searched, she must have gone to the fire, stripped the 'glove' off, and burned it. But leather never burns easily. I would guess that she dipped it in his brandy first, which is quite combustible. It was a hot fire, but I imagine you could find a little hard lump of it in the ashes, if you knew what you were looking for."

"Not that it matters now."

"No, it doesn't matter any more."

"What if somebody had touched the knife when you first found him and messed up the prints?"

"It isn't likely they would all have been lost. But she must have been ready to say, 'Don't touch anything until the police get here.' "

"Risky."

"Well, if the prints had been smeared, what would have happened? We would have had a problem. We might think she was the person most likely to have done it or we might not have, but with eight people there, how could you know for sure? The knife was her father's and available to anybody there, which even allowed for an impulse murder. The manuscript could have been a motive for that. But what she preferred was not a guessing game with everybody suspected including herself. She wanted to prove that someone from outside had done it. And she just barely failed."

"You told me once you didn't believe she wanted his money."

"I didn't and I don't believe she did. I also said murders were done out of hatred, remember? Do you realize what the girl went through, growing up in that house? It would have been better if there had been a son as well. Not great, but better. She would simply have had a cold father to put up with. But the way it was, she was the disappointment. The girl who should have been a boy. The thing that wasn't good enough. She devoted herself to her father, trying to win his approval. She waited on him. She went into his profession. At the same time, she had too much basic honesty to agree with everything he said, and he did not like that. We have no record of his ever showing her any approval. No tenderness. Nothing. Then, on their standing argument of what to do about hopeless patients, look what Cotton did to her. He told her that two patients at Hastings Hospital who had looked hopeless had in fact recovered. And she used that data from him in an article she was working on and which was later published. Then he, in effect, said, 'Ha! They didn't survive after all. This will show you that you should always check out your facts.' But check your own father for treachery? Alec told us about this. Cotton no doubt made himself believe he was teaching her an important lesson about research. But she must have known it was another expression of his sadistic nature. And a desire to win the argument, no matter what the methods. Then came the real blow. He was planning to use the same two cases in an article, which would thoroughly discredit her in print among those who knew—admittedly a small number. But it was too much. At that point she turned. She behaved the same to him outwardly, but from then on, inwardly, she felt only hatred for him. She planned how to kill him.''

She had plenty of time. He published about one article a year. He was a methodical worker. He had the manuscript there that night to give her an additional needling, but she had known of it for months.

And it was hardly even the important thing any more. Getting rid of him was."

"You can almost sympathize with her when you put it that way."

"Yes, and I'm sure that was how Erikson felt. I think as soon as it happened he knew who must have done it, if not how. So after the murder he tried to get into the room to get the manuscript and destroy it before we read it."

"But he couldn't get to it."

"No, and anyhow we had heard about Cotton's trick from Alec as well. We had the impression that Melanie sort of dropped Erikson after the murder, but really it was just the other way around. He was sorry for her, he would have tried to protect her, but he just didn't feel the same toward her after that. He is an unusually soft-hearted, sympathetic person, I think. It was he, you know, who tried hardest to console Aunt Helen when she was so distraught. Actually, we never saw him do anything but kind-hearted things. The scars on his hands, for instance. He wouldn't talk about them, but I found out he got them when an oxygen tent caught fire and he pulled the child out from under it with his bare hands. Not part of our problem, of course. It was he who took the unknown bridge player, Passim, for a partner when Passim was feeling lonely and worried. Erikson even wanted to help our gravediggers. He must have known what Cotton was like, in the way an opposite sort of person can understand. I had to take him along to see Clarence Scott's body, because he had to come to terms with himself about Melanie. He had to see that there was no possibility of mistake, because he had to give her up totally, not go around in an unhappy, ambivalent daze, as he had since the murder."

"Why was she so eager to help you test out prints and so on?"

"Melanie did not start tagging along until she heard me say that I was unsatisfied with your analysis, that it had to have been somebody in the room. That was in your office. Then she knew she was in trouble. She wanted to keep an eye on me. You know, when she tried out the knife for Lumpkins, her fingers fitted it the same way the murderer's had. My thumb went a little farther along. She never actually stated or tried to prove that any specific person had killed her father, except a dead man. I think that finding Johns and Pryczyk in the hall was a terrific blow to her. After that, she had to latch on to whatever source of information was handy. I was handy."

The way he said it did not tell me how he felt.

"By the way," I said, "I heard that Erikson has just started work on some sort of implanted dialysis device. It's supposed to make it possible for the patient to go about his daily business while his blood is being cleaned and it ought to cost a lot less than hospital dialysis, too."

"Good for him."

"Alec Spruance turned up at my office that afternoon. He hadn't heard about Melanie. He'd come to tell us that Dr. Passim was the killer and we could prove it if we only worked at it."

"Did he say why?"

"Alec had been going around the hospital detecting. He talked to Passim, who made the mistake of showing him some coin tricks he'd been practicing. Making coins vanish, that kind of thing. He was doing it to improve his dexterity for surgery, he told

Alec, but Alec was too clever to believe that, of course."

"And he used some sort of magic to cause the fingerprints to fly to the knife?"

"Something like that. Fuzzy thinking is everywhere."

"How is Mrs. Coyne?"

"There's good and bad news. She's conscious and recovering. But they say it isn't likely she'll ever be able to use her left leg again. She doesn't seem at all despondent about that. She says she's lucky to be alive and always plays bridge sitting down, anyhow."

"Mmm. Did she say what happened to her?"

"She was waiting for the bus on the corner in front of the hospital, chatting with Melanie Cotton. After that she doesn't remember anything at all."

# THE EYES ON
# UTOPIA MURDERS
### by
### Award-Winning Author
### Barbara D'Amato

Visit us at www.speakingvolumes.us

"Edgy, surprising, and spiced with rich characterizations."
—*Publishers Weekly*

"Slam-bang adventure and suspense. Readers expect
no less from D'Amato." —*Chicago Sun-Times*

Visit us at www.speakingvolumes.us

# WHITE MALE INFANT
## by
## Award-Winning Author
## Barbara D'Amato

"Another D'Amato stunner... D'Amato knows how to wring suspense out of her subjects... Fraught with tension... complex but riveting."
—*Booklist*

WHITE MALE INFANT

BARBARA D'AMATO

Published by SpeakingVolumes

Visit us at www.speakingvolumes.us

GREAT BOOKS

E-BOOKS

AUDIOBOOKS

& MORE

Visit us today